HAVE A HIGHLAND
M. C. BEATON'S

#5 Hamish McBeth

"...h."

Marilyn Stasio, New York Times
Book Review

"Reading Beaton is an experience akin to discovering buried treasure... An outstanding read from one of the real masters of mystery."

—*Booklist* (starred review)

"Macbeth's charm continues to grow... Fun, silly, and as light as a well-made scone—I wouldn't miss a single book."

—*Christian Science Monitor*

"The detective novels of M. C. Beaton, a master of outrageous black comedy... have reached cult status in the United States."

—*The Times Magazine* (London)

"Inspired... satisfying fun... Hamish is a gem."

—*Kirkus Reviews*

"Engrossing, cozy mystery...with residents and a constable so authentic it won't be long before tourists will be seeking Lochdubh and believing in the reality of Hamish Macbeth as surely as they believed in Sherlock Holmes."

—Denver Rocky Mountain News

"Befuddled, earnest, and utterly endearing, Hamish makes his triumphs sweetly satisfying."

—Publishers Weekly

"Macbeth is the sort of character who slyly grows on you...as you realize that beneath his unassuming exterior, he's a whiz at cutting through all the hokum."

—Chicago Sun-Times

"Beaton's plot and characters are as splendidly cast as the scenic backdrop she has chosen for Lochdubh."

—Des Moines Sunday Register (IA)

Death *of a* Hussy

Previous Hamish Macbeth Mysteries by M. C. Beaton

M.C. BEATON

Death *of a* Hussy

GC

GRAND CENTRAL
PUBLISHING

NEW YORK   BOSTON

Copyright © 1990 by M. C. Beaton
Excerpt from *Death of a Policeman* copyright © 2013 by Marion Chesney
Excerpt from *Death of Yesterday* copyright © 2013 by Marion Chesney
Excerpt from *Death of a Nag* copyright © 2013 by Marion Chesney

Grand Central Publishing
Hachette Book Group
1290 Avenue of the Americas
New York, NY 10104
www.HachetteBookGroup.com

Grand Central Publishing is a division of Hachette Book Group, Inc. The Grand Central Publishing name and logo is a trademark of Hachette Book Group, Inc.

The Hachette Speakers Bureau provides a wide range of authors for speaking events. To find out more, go to www.hachettespeakersbureau.com or call (866) 376-6591.

The publisher is not responsible for websites (or their content) that are not owned by the publisher.

Printed in the United States of America

First Grand Central Publishing mass market edition: August 2013

10 9 8 7 6 5 4 3 2

OPM

The author wishes to thank Hugh Johnston, owner and manager of Golspie Motors Ltd., of Golspie, Sutherland, his service manager, John Mackay, and his mechanic, Bill Brown, for their expert advice, and dedicates this book with gratitude to these three excellent and patient gentlemen of the Scottish Highlands.

Death *of a* Hussy

Chapter One

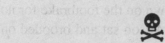

In the Highlands in the country places
Where the old plain men have rosy faces,
And the young fair maidens
Quiet eyes.

—R. L. Stevenson

"You might have known people really do dress up for dinner in the Highlands." Maggie Baird shifted her large bulk irritably in the driving seat and crashed the gears horribly.

Beside her in the passenger seat of the battered Renault 5, her niece, Alison Kerr, sat in miserable silence. Her aunt Maggie had already gone on and on and *on* about Alison's shabby appearance before they left the house. Alison had tried to protest that, had she been warned about this dinner invitation to Tommel Castle, she would have washed and set her hair and possibly bought a new dress. As it was, her black hair was lank and greasy and she wore a plain navy skirt and a white blouse.

As Maggie Baird mangled the car on its way to Tommel Castle—that is, she seemed to wrench the gears a lot and stamp down on the footbrake for no apparent reason at all—Alison sat and brooded on her bad luck.

Life had seemed to take on new hope and meaning when her mother's sister, Maggie Baird, had descended on the hospital where Alison was recovering from lung cancer in Bristol. Alison's parents were both dead. She had, when they were alive, heard little about this Mrs. Maggie Baird, except, "We don't talk about her, dear, and want to have nothing to do with her."

When she had thought she was about to die, Alison had written to Maggie. After all, Maggie appeared to be her only surviving relative and there should be at least one person to arrange the funeral. Maggie had swept into the patient's lounge, exuding a strong air of maternal warmth. Alison would come with her to her new home in the Highlands and convalesce.

And so Alison had been borne off to Maggie's large sprawling bungalow home on the hills overlooking the sea outside the village of Lochdubh in Sutherland in the very north of Scotland.

The first week had been pleasant. The bungalow was overcarpeted, overwarm, and overfurnished. But there was an efficient housekeeper—what in the old days would have been called a maid of all work—who came up from the village every day to clean and cook. This treasure was called Mrs. Todd and although Alison was thirty-one, Mrs. Todd treated her like a little girl and made her special cakes for afternoon tea.

By the second week Alison longed to escape from the house. Maggie herself went down to the village to do the shopping but she would never take Alison. Eventually all that maternal warmth faded, to be replaced by a carping bitchiness. Alison, still feeling weak and dazed and gutless after her recent escape from death, could not stand up to her aunt and endured the increasing insults in a morose silence.

Then had come the invitation to dinner from the Halburton-Smythes, local landowners, who lived out on the far side of the village at Tommel Castle, and Maggie had not told her about their going until the very last minute, hence the lank hair and the blouse and skirt.

Maggie crashed the gears again as they went up a steep hill. Alison winced. What a way to treat a car! If she herself could only drive! Oh, to be able to go racing up and over the mountains and to be free and not immured in the centrally heated prison that was Maggie's bungalow. Of course, Alison should just leave and get a job somewhere, but the doctors had told her to take it easy for at least six months and somehow she felt too drained of energy to even try to escape from Maggie. She was terrified of a recurrence of cancer. It was all very well for other people to point out that these days cancer need not be a terminal illness. Alison had had a small part of her lung removed. She was terribly aware of it, imagining a great hole lurking inside her chest. She longed daily for a cigarette and often refused to believe that a diet of forty cigarettes a day had contributed to her illness.

Maggie swung the little red car between two imposing gate posts and up a well-kept drive.

Alison braced herself. What would these people be like?

PRISCILLA HALBURTON-SMYTHE PUSHED the food around her plate and wished the evening would end. She did not like Maggie Baird, who, resplendent in a huge green and gold caftan, was eating with relish. Her voice was "county" as she talked to Colonel Halburton-Smythe about the iniquities of poachers, and only Alison knew that Maggie had a talent for sounding knowledgeable on all sorts of subjects she knew little about.

I can't quite make her out, thought Priscilla. She's a great fat woman and quite nasty to that little niece of hers and yet Daddy is going on like an Edwardian gallant. He seems quite taken with her.

She looked again at Alison. Alison Kerr was a thin girl—well, possibly in her thirties, but such a waif that it was hard to think of her as a woman. She had thick horn-rimmed glasses, and her black hair fell in two wings shielding most of her face. She had very good skin, very pale, almost translucent. Priscilla flashed a smile at Alison who scowled and looked at her plate.

Priscilla was everything Alison despised. She was beautiful in a cool poised way with shining pale gold hair worn in a simple style. Her scarlet silk dress with the ruffled Spanish sleeves must have cost a fortune. Her voice was charming and amused.

I would be charming and amused if I lived in a castle and had doting parents, thought Alison bitterly. I know what that smile meant. She's sorry for me. Damn her.

"You will find you have to do a lot of driving in the Highlands, Mrs. Baird," the colonel said.

Maggie sighed and then looked at him with a

wicked twinkle in her eyes. "How true," she said. "I'm up and down that road to the village like a tart's drawers."

There was a little silence. Mrs. Halburton-Smythe opened her mouth a little and then shut it again. Then the colonel gave an indulgent laugh. "It's not London," he said. "There isn't an Asian grocer at the corner of every field. You have to make lists, you know. It's quite possible to buy all the groceries for a week in one go. Doesn't that housekeeper of yours do the shopping?"

"I prefer to do it myself," said Maggie, once more falling into the role of country gentlewoman. "I like to get the best of everything although Lochdubh is pretty limited. I think the inhabitants must live on a diet of fish fingers."

"You should take a trip into Inverness and stock up," said Mrs. Halburton-Smythe. "They've got everything there now. Quite a boom town and expanding every day. Why, I remember not so long ago when it was a sleepy place and they drove the Highland cattle to market through the main street. Now it's all cars, cars, cars."

"And crime on the increase," said the colonel. "What those fools in Strathbane think they're about to leave us without a policeman, I don't know."

"Hamish!" said Priscilla. "You didn't tell me."

She smiled at Alison. "I only arrived last night and haven't caught up with the local news. Hamish gone? Where?"

"They've closed down the police station and taken that lazy lout off to Strathbane," said her father. "It's funny, I never thought Macbeth actually did anything. Now he's gone and someone has been netting salmon in the river. At least Macbeth would have found a way to stop it, although he never arrested anyone."

"But this is dreadful," exclaimed Priscilla. "Hamish is a terrible loss to the village."

"Well, *you* would naturally think so," said her father acidly.

Priscilla's cool manner seemed ruffled. Oho! thought Alison, I wonder if the daughter of the castle is in love with the absent local copper.

Maggie looked amused. "If you want to get him back," she said, "all you need to do is manufacture some crime in the village."

She flashed a flirtatious look at the colonel. Priscilla thought, It's as if there's a beauty encased under that layer of fat.

But she said aloud, "What a good idea. Why don't we organise a meeting in the village hall and put it to the locals."

The colonel seemed about to protest but the

suggestion caught Maggie's imagination. She liked to imagine herself a leader of Highland village society.

"I'll arrange it for you if you like," she said. "Alison can help. Or try to help. She's not really good at anything, you know. When shall we have the meeting?"

"Why not this Saturday?" asked Priscilla.

"You are not suggesting you are going to encourage the villagers to commit crimes so as to get Hamish back!" said Mrs. Halburton-Smythe.

"Something must be done," said Priscilla. "We'll put it to the locals and then take a vote."

"A vote on what?" demanded her father.

"On whatever suggestions are put up," said Priscilla evasively. "There's no need for you to get involved, Daddy. I am sure Mrs. Baird and I can handle everything."

Alison found herself beginning to speculate on this local bobby. He must be someone very special to attract the cool Priscilla. Her mind wandered off into fantasy. What if she helped to get him back, managed to do more than Priscilla? This Hamish Macbeth would be tall and fair and handsome like those paintings of Bonnie Prince Charlie on the old biscuit tins. He would fall in love with her, Alison, and take her away from Maggie and leave Priscilla with the knowledge that Alison's inner attractions were more important to a man than stereotyped outward beauty. She lacks character in her face, thought Alison, looking under her lashes at Priscilla and trying to find fault.

At last the evening was over. Maggie was wrapped by the butler in a voluminous mink coat. I hope Macbeth isn't into Animal Liberation, thought Alison maliciously. That coat must have taken a whole ranch of minks.

As she was leaving, the colonel suddenly leaned forward and kissed Maggie on the cheek. She flashed him a roguish look and he puffed out his chest and strutted like a bantam.

Oh, dear, thought Priscilla, I wish he wouldn't make such a fool of himself.

She did not know that her father's misplaced gallantry was to start a chain of events which would lead to murder.

MAGGIE WAS IN a good mood as she drove home through the wintry landscape and under the bright and burning stars of Sutherland. So she could still attract a man. And if she could attract a man when she was like this—well, plump—think what effect she could have if she took herself in hand.

It was all the fault of that damned waiter, thought

Maggie. Maggie Baird had earned a considerable amount of money during her career. Although she had managed to stay off the streets and had been married and divorced twice, she had made a business out of being mistress to a long string of wealthy men, occasionally straying to the poorer ones for her own amusement. Like most women addicted to food, she also had a tremendous appetite for sex. Unlike most of her sisters on the game, she had squirreled away her earnings, buying and selling property and investing cleverly. That was when the blow had fallen. Finding herself a very wealthy woman and looking for amusement, Maggie had taken up with a Greek waiter whose swarthy good looks had appealed to her. But for the first time in her life, she had fallen helplessly in love and when she had found that he was taking her money to save enough to marry a young blonde from Stepney, she felt her life was over.

She had bought the bungalow in the Highlands, a place to lick her wounds. She had let the bleach grow out of her hair so that it became its natural brown streaked with grey. She had put on pounds and pounds in weight. She wore tweeds and suede hats and oilskin coats and brogues and everything she could to adopt the character of a Scottish gentlewoman, as if hiding her hurt under layers of fat and country dress.

Taking Alison out of the hospital made her feel good for a while, until the novelty had worn off. Now the pain of the waiter's rejection was fading as well.

"There's life in the old girl yet," she said cheerfully.

"You mean the car?" asked Alison.

"Me, you fool, not this heap of junk."

"It's a very nice little car," said Alison timidly. "Auntie—"

"I told you not to call me that," snapped Maggie.

"Sorry...Maggie. Look, do you think I could take driving lessons? I could do the shopping for you."

"I've got more to do with my money than pay for your driving lessons," said Maggie. "That colonel's quite a lad. His wife looks a bit of a faded nonentity. And that daughter of his! No character."

"Exactly," agreed Alison eagerly. Both women fell to trashing Priscilla and arrived home quite pleased with each other for the first time in weeks.

THE HIGHLANDS OF Scotland contain many pretty towns and villages but Strathbane was not one of them. It had been attractive once, but had become a centre for light industry in the early fifties and that had brought people flooding in from the cities. Ugly housing complexes had been thrown up all round; garish supermarkets, discos, and wine bars and all the doubtful benefits of a booming economy had come to Strathbane along with crime and drugs.

Police Constable Hamish Macbeth sadly left the kennels where his dog, Towser, was housed. It was his evening off. He was bored and lonely and he hated Strathbane and he hated Detective Chief Inspector Blair with a passion for moving him out of Lochdubh.

He was sick and tired of the youth of Strathbane with their white pinched faces, their drunkenness, and their obscenities. He was tired of raiding discos for drugs, and bars for drunks, and football matches for hooligans.

He walked along the dirty streets. A thin drizzle was falling. Even the seagulls wheeling under the harsh orange light of the sodium street lamps looked dirty. He leaned on the wall and stared down on the beach. The tide was up; oil glittered on the water and an old sofa with burst springs was slowly being gathered in by the rising tide.

A man reeled past him, then leaned against the sea wall and vomited onto the beach. Hamish shuddered and moved away. He wondered how much longer he could endure this existence. His home in Lochdubh had been the police station, so he did not even have a house to go back to. The neighbours were looking after his hens and his sheep, but he could not expect them to do so indefinitely. Some real estate agent would probably sell the police station. He had left most of his possessions there, refusing to believe his life in Lochdubh was over.

Then there was Mary Graham. P.C. Graham was Hamish's usual partner on the beat in Strathbane. She was a thin, spare woman with a hard face and dyed blond hair and a thirst for making as many arrests as possible. She was from the south of Scotland and considered Hamish some sort of half-witted peasant.

Hamish's mind went back and forth and round and round the problem, seeking escape. He could always go back to Lochdubh and take lodgings with someone. He could move his hen houses onto the bit of croft land assigned to him. But, like all crofters, he knew it was impossible to live on small farming alone, trying to wrest a living out of a few stony fields. He could work on the fishing boats, of course.

What hurt most of all was that the people of Lochdubh appeared to have taken his banishment without comment. He felt very friendless.

ON SATURDAY NIGHT, the village hall in Lochdubh was crammed to capacity. On the platform facing the audience was the committee made up of Maggie, Alison, Priscilla, and the minister, Mr. Wellington, and his large, tweedy wife—who for the first time in her life was outdone in largeness and tweediness. Maggie Baird was encased in new tweeds and had a suede hat with a pheasant's feather on it on her head. Alison had washed and set her hair for the occasion, perhaps in the hope that the handsome policeman would walk in the door while the meeting was on.

Maggie Baird, much to the annoyance of Mrs. Wellington, rose to speak.

"Our local policeman has been sent away because of a lack of crime in the area. I suggest we organise enough crime to make it necessary to send him back."

There was a roar of approval. Shocked, Mrs. Wellington struggled to her feet and held up her hands for silence.

"That is a most dreadful and, if you will forgive me, Mrs. Baird, *immoral* suggestion."

"What would you suggest?" asked Maggie with dangerous sweetness.

"Well, I think we should get up a petition."

"We'll put it to a vote," said Maggie. "All in favour of organising some crime, raise their hands."

A forest of hands went up.

"All in favour of a petition?"

Only a few hands went up.

Mr. Wellington took the floor. "You cannot, Mrs. Baird, expect us all to break the law."

"No one said anything about breaking the law," replied Maggie cheerfully. "We make it look as if we've got a crime and insist on having the police in. I am going to pass round sheets of paper and you will all write down suggestions. I will report that something of mine, something valuable, has been stolen, and then after a bit I'll say, 'Sorry to have wasted your time, it has been found.' That sort of thing."

There was a silence in the hall. Maggie realised furiously that everyone was obviously waiting for Priscilla to say something.

Feudal lot of peasants, thought Maggie angrily.

Priscilla got to her feet. She was wearing a smart grey tailored pin-striped suit with a white blouse, sheer stockings, and patent leather high heels. "Yes, I think a bit of organised crime is the sensible answer," said Priscilla. "My father is having trouble again with poachers. I shall start off with that complaint."

There was a cheer and a man shouted, "Good for you. We knew you would think of something."

In that moment, Alison felt quite warm toward

her aunt. It did seem unfair that Maggie should have thought up the scheme only to have everyone give Priscilla all the credit.

Papers were passed around, a few half bottles of whisky were produced, the villagers scribbled busily. The air was soon heavy with the raw smell of alcohol and a fog of cigarette smoke.

When the meeting was over, everyone was happy with the results—with the exception of Mr. and Mrs. Wellington, Maggie, and Alison.

"Why did I bother?" fumed Maggie on the road home. "Did you see that Halburton-Smythe bitch calmly taking the credit for everything? Anyway, my crime is the best and so I shall show them."

SERGEANT MACGREGOR DROVE angrily over the twisting Highland roads that led from Cnothan to Lochdubh. Some female had lost her diamond earrings and what should have been handled by that Macbeth fellow was now having to be handled by him, MacGregor.

What made it worse was that this female, this Mrs. Baird, had phoned the high-ups in Strathbane and accused them of deliberately encouraging crime in Lochdubh by taking away the village policeman and had threatened to write to *The Times*.

He drove through Lochdubh, remarking sourly

to himself that it looked as sleepy as ever, and took the coast road to Maggie's bungalow.

The door was opened by a grim-looking house-keeper wearing a blue cotton dress with a white collar. MacGregor's heart sank. Anyone who could afford to employ a Scottish housekeeper these days and get her to wear a sort of uniform must be stinking rich, and stinking rich meant power, and power meant trouble.

Mrs. Baird was all he had feared and anticipated. She was a great, fat woman wearing a tweed suit and heavy brogues. Her thick hair was scraped back in an old-fashioned bun and she had the glacial accents of the upper class. With her on the chintz-covered sofa sat a dab of a woman, peering at him through thick-lensed glasses, whom Mrs. Baird introduced as "my niece, Miss Kerr."

"You took your time about getting here," said Maggie.

"Well, I have to come from Cnothan, which is a good wee bit away," said MacGregor with what he hoped was a placating smile.

"Stop grinning like a monkey and get your notebook out," ordered Maggie. The housekeeper brought in a tray with a coffee pot, cream, sugar, and only two cups. MacGregor was obviously not going to be offered any.

"When did you first notice the earrings were missing?" asked MacGregor.

"Last night. I've searched the house. Mrs. Todd, the housekeeper, is a local woman and above suspicion. But two suspicious-looking hikers were seen hanging about yesterday. They could have got in somehow and taken them."

"Description?" asked MacGregor, licking his pencil.

"Man and a girl, early twenties. The man had a straggly beard and the girl looked like one of those dreary intellectual types, rather like Miss Kerr here." Maggie laughed and Alison winced. "The man was wearing a camouflage jacket and jeans, and the girl, a red anorak and brown slacks. The man had on a ski cap and the girl was hatless. Her hair was mousy brown."

MacGregor eventually drove off in a more cheerful frame of mind. He had something concrete to go on. He telephoned from his Land Rover to Strathbane and put out an alert for the hikers. That strange creature, Macbeth, who had had the temerity to solve a murder case in his, MacGregor's, absence, would soon find out his presence was not missed in Lochdubh.

He had only just reached home when a call came through from the chief constable. Colonel

DEATH OF A HUSSY 19

Halburton-Smythe demanded the presence of a policeman immediately. Poachers were netting salmon on his river. With a groan, MacGregor set out for Lochdubh again. The colonel insisted on taking the sergeant on a long walk across country to the river and haranguing him on the ineptitude of the police. MacGregor was tired and weary by the time he got back to Cnothan.

But fury gave him energy, fury generated by a call from Strathbane to say that Mrs. Baird had telephoned. She had found her lost earrings down the back of the sofa and what was MacGregor doing wasting the force's time by having them look for villainous hikers who did not exist?

Then a phone call came from the Lochdubh Hotel to say that a group of young people were creating a riot in the public bar. MacGregor appealed for back-up and took the road back to Lochdubh to find the public bar empty apart from a few shattered glasses and the owner of the hotel, who was unable to give a clear description of the young people.

By the time he finally got home to bed, he was nearly in tears of rage. Morning found him in a calmer frame of mind. Lochdubh would sink back into its usual peace and quiet.

And then the phone started to ring. A crofter in Lochdubh complained that five of his sheep had

been stolen during the night, and a farmer reported
that two of his prize cows were missing. The schoolteacher, Miss Monson, called to say that drugs had
been found in a classroom.

Again MacGregor telephoned for help, only to
be asked wearily why he couldn't handle things
himself—that is, until he got to the tale of the drugs
in the classroom. Detective Chief Inspector Blair
and a team of detectives and forensic men were des-
patched from Strathbane only to find that the drugs
in the classroom were packets of baking soda. "Silly
me," said the giggling schoolteacher, and Blair took
his anger out on MacGregor, who had no one to take
it out on except his wife, and he was afraid of her.

THE AMAZING THING about British policewomen
is that a surprising proportion of them are attractive. And so P.C. Hamish Macbeth could not help
wondering why he had the ill luck to be saddled
with such a creature as Mary Graham on his beat.
P.C. Graham, he reflected, looked like one of those
women you see in German war films. Not only was
there the dyed blond hair, but she had staring ice-
blue eyes, a mouth like a trap, and an impeccable
uniform with a short tailored skirt which showed
strong muscular legs encased in black tights—
not fine sheer tights worn by some of the younger

policewomen, but thick wool ones, and her shoes were like black polished glass.

It was a sunny day as they walked side by side along the waterfront, past closed bars smelling of last night's drunks; past shuttered warehouses falling into ruin, relics of the days when Strathbane was a small busy port; past blocks of houses thrown up in the fifties during that period when all architects seem to have sold their souls to Stalin, and had erected towers of concrete very like their counterparts in Moscow. The balconies had once been painted jolly primary colours, but now long trails of rust ran down the cracked concrete of the buildings in which elevators had long since died, and rubbish lay in heaps on the sour earth of what was originally intended to be a communal garden.

"I always keep ma eyes and ears open," Mary was saying. She had a whining singsong voice. "I hae noticed, Macbeth, you're apt to turn a blind eye tae too many things."

"Such as?" asked Hamish while in his mind he picked her up and threw her over the sea wall and then watched her sink slowly beneath the oily surface of the rising tide.

"Two days ago there were these two drunks fighting outside The Glen bar. All you did was separate them and send them off home. I wanted to arrest them and would hae done had I not seen that wee boy acting suspiciously over at the supermarket."

Hamish sighed. There was no point replying. Mary saw villains everywhere. But her next words nearly roused him to a fury, and it took a great deal to rouse Hamish Macbeth. "I felt it was ma duty to put in a report about you," she said. "It is cramping my style to have to walk the beat wi' a Highland layabout. The trouble wi' you Highlanders is you just want to lie on your backs all day long. You know whit they say, *mañana* is too *urgent* a word for you." Mary laughed merrily at her own wit. "So I said I would never rise in the force, having to patrol wi' a deadbeat like you, and asked for a change."

"That would be nice," said Hamish.

Mary threw him a startled look. "I'm surprised you're taking it so well."

"Of course I am taking it well. Ye dinnae think I enjoy walking along on a fine day wi' a sour-faced bitch like you," said Hamish in a light pleasant voice, although Priscilla, for example, would have recognised, by the sudden sibilancy of it, that Hamish was furious. "Wass I not saying chust the other day," said Hamish dreamily, "that it was sore luck getting landed wi' you instead of someone like Pat Macleod." Pat Macleod was a curvaceous brunette of a police-woman who wore sheer stockings

instead of tights. Every policeman who had seen her
flashing her thighs in the canteen as she deliberately
hitched up her short skirt to sit down could bear
witness to that.

Mary could hardly believe her ears. She would
never for a moment have dreamt that P.C. Macbeth
would even think of insulting her. She did not know
that her contempt for him was largely based on jealousy. Macbeth, in a short time, had made himself
popular on the beat and householders preferred to
bring their troubles to him rather than to Mary.

"I have never been so insulted in all my life," she
said.

"Oh, come now, wi' a face and manner like
yours, you must have been," said Hamish who, like
all normally polite and kind people, was relishing
the rarity of being truly and thoroughly rude.

"You're jist mad because Blair winkled ye oot
o' your cosy number in Lochdubh," sneered Mary.
"And you claim to have solved them murders! You!
You're no' a man. I could beat the living daylights
oot o' you any day."

"Try it," said Hamish.

She squared up to him. "I warn ye. I'm a black
belt in karate."

"Behave yourself, woman," said Hamish, suddenly sick to death of her.

With amazing speed, he moved in under her guard, swept her up in his lanky arms, dumped her head first in an enormous plastic rubbish bin, and, deaf to her cries, strolled off.

That's that, he thought with gloomy satisfaction, I may as well go back to the police station and resign.

The desk sergeant looked up as Hamish ambled in. "Upstairs, Macbeth. The super's screaming for you."

"So soon?" said Hamish, surprised. "Did P.C. Graham fly in on her broomstick? Never mind. Better get it over with."

"Come in, come in, Hamish," said Superintendent Peter Daviot. "Sit down, man. Tea?"

"Yes, thank you," said Hamish, sitting down on a chair facing the desk and putting his peaked cap on his knees.

"It seems, Hamish, that there's been a bit of a crime wave in Lochdubh and Sergeant MacGregor's being run ragged."

"Is he now?" asked Hamish with a smile. He did not like MacGregor.

"Milk and sugar? Right. Here you are. Yes, on due consideration, we have decided you should finish up the week here and return to Lochdubh. Here are the keys to the station."

"Thank you." Hamish felt suddenly bleak. Why had he risen to that stupid Graham woman's insults?

The door opened and Detective Chief Inspector Blair heaved his large bulk into the room. "Oh, you're here, are you?" he said nastily when he saw Hamish.

"Yes," said Mr. Daviot. "It seems you made a bad mistake in suggesting that Hamish be taken away from Lochdubh. There's been nothing but crime for the past few days."

"I know," said Blair heavily. "I've been there on a drugs report. Baking soda, it turned oot tae be." His Glasgow accent grew stronger in his irritation. "Dae ye know what I think? I think them damp villagers are making up crimes so as tae get this pillock back."

The superintendent's face froze. "Mind your language in front of me, Mr. Blair," he said. "Are you questioning the word of Colonel Halburton-Smythe, for example?"

"No, no," said Blair hurriedly. "But it did look a bit suspicious, ye ken, considering nothing happens there from the one year's end tae the other."

"Except murder," put in Hamish.

"Do not forget Hamish solved that woman's murder," said the superintendent. "I am just telling him he must go back and take up his duties there."

"Uh-uh!" said Blair, his face creased into an unlovely smile. "Why I came up, Mr. Daviot, is to tell you we might be discussing Macbeth's dismissal from the force."

"What! Why?"

"He assaulted P.C. Graham."

"You assaulted a policewoman, Hamish?"

"It was self-defence, sir."

"Haw! Haw! Haw!" roared Blair.

"Will you stop cackling, Blair, and give me an outline of the complaint?"

"P.C. Graham has just come into the station. She said she was patrolling the beat when Macbeth here suddenly picked her up and threw her in a rubbish bin."

"Is this true, Macbeth?" No more "Hamish."

"She said she could beat me up and approached me in a threatening manner," said Hamish. "I was fed up wi' her. I chust picked up the lassie and dumped her in wi' the garbage."

"I can hardly...this is very serious...very serious indeed. Oh, what is it, Sergeant?"

The desk sergeant had just entered. "It's three women and a man frae the tower blocks," he said. "They say they've come to defend Macbeth here. They say they saw Graham attacking him and Macbeth being forced to defend himself. They say when

they helped Graham out of the bin, she said she was
going to get Macbeth charged with assault and they
say if that's the case they will all go to court as wit-
nesses for Macbeth's defence."

"We must not let this get into the newspapers,"
said the superintendent, horrified. "Get rid of these
people, Sergeant, and say that Macbeth is not being
charged. Shut Graham up at all costs. Good heav-
ens, just think what the tabloids could make of this.
Macbeth, I suggest you go back to your quarters
and pack and leave for Lochdubh in the morning.
Blair, I am surprised at you! In a situation as poten-
tially explosive and damaging to the police as this
you should get your facts right. Macbeth, wipe that
smile off your face and get going!"

Chapter Two

And with the morn those angel faces smile,
Which I have loved long since, and lost awhile.

—Cardinal John Henry Newman

At a new roundabout on the outskirts of Strathbane stood Hamish Macbeth, a suitcase in one hand. In the other, he held a rope as a leash for Towser, whose own had mysteriously disappeared in the kennels. Towser, a yellowish mongrel, was subdued. He had been kennelled with police dogs, large nasty-looking German shepherds, and had lived for a short time in a state of terror.

There was no reason for Hamish to be standing in a fine drizzle trying to hitch a lift. A police car would have driven him to Lochdubh in the afternoon, but Hamish felt he could not wait that long.

One car after another slowed at the roundabout and then drove past the solitary figure with the battered suitcase and dog. Many people firmly believed you had to have a death wish to give a lift to a stranger these days.

Hamish looked around. There was a thick stand of bushes behind him. He walked into their shelter, opened his case, took out his policeman's tunic, and after tugging off his old sweater, put it on. He was already wearing his regulation trousers. He also fished out his peaked hat and knocked it back into shape and put it on his head.

"I told you, you shouldn't be driving without a licence," said Mrs. Mary Webb to her husband, Bert, as the tall, thin figure of a policeman stepped out into the road just before the roundabout and held up his hand. Bert Webb slowed to a halt, his heart hammering. "Whatever happens, keep your mouth shut," he hissed to his wife.

He rolled down the window. "Good day, Officer," he said with an ingratiating leer. "What can we do for you?"

"I was wondering if you were travelling any-where near the village of Lochdubh," said Hamish.

"We are going farther north," said Bert uneasily. "The nearest we get to Lochdubh is the Ardest crossroads."

"That would do me just fine," said Hamish. "I can walk from there easily."

A look of relief wiped the worry from Bert's face. "You mean you want a lift?"

"If you would be so kind."

Relief made Bert hearty. "Jump in the back," he said.

"Thank you very much," said Hamish with a sweet smile. "I will just be getting my dog." And he disappeared back into the bushes beside the road where he had left Towser.

"Dog!" exclaimed Mary Webb. "And us with our new seat covers." She twisted her head and looked at the back seat which was covered in imitation fur fabric of a leopard skin pattern.

"Shut up!" snapped Bert, uneasy again. "It may be some sort of trick."

His wife looked at him in alarm but had no time to say anything, for the back door of the car opened and P.C. Macbeth and a wet Towser climbed inside, Hamish pulling his suitcase in after him.

Hamish tried to make conversation but found it very hard going. Mary Webb was thinking furiously, Perhaps it isn't Bert's licence, perhaps it's those library books I never took back. Then there was that restaurant. They forgot to charge Bert for the drinks and he never said a word....

Bert was thinking of the young girl with whom he had enjoyed a brief fling down in Worcester three months ago. He was a shop fitter and travelled around the country. The girl had looked awfully young. What if she was under sixteen?

Hamish finally fell silent. His thoughts turned to Lochdubh. He was still saddened by the way in which all his friends had taken his banishment without any fuss. He had phoned the hotel the night before and had told Mr. Johnson, the manager, of his imminent return and Johnson had taken it calmly, almost coolly, in fact.

"Here we are, Officer!" said Bert with forced joviality. "The Ardest turning."

Hamish thanked them and climbed out with suitcase and dog. He touched his cap as the Webbs drove off, the Webbs who were now full of indignant rage at having been forced to give a lift to what had turned out to be nothing more sinister than a scrounging copper.

Towser turned slowly in the direction of Lochdubh, rather like an overstuffed armchair turning around on its castors. He sniffed the air and slowly his tail curved over his back.

A shaft of sunlight struck through the grey clouds, a William Blake shaft of sunlight. All it lacked were the angels. The wind was from the west holding an underlying touch of warmth. Above the shaggy heath of Sutherland soared the mountains, rising up to heaven, away and beyond the antlike machinations of the police force.

Hamish took the rope from around Towser's neck and the dog surged forward down the road to Loch-dubh, stopping every now and then to look back and make sure his master was following.

Hoisting his suitcase up onto his shoulder, Hamish stepped out smartly and the sky above grew brighter and brighter and the wind in the heather sang a welcome home.

"THANK GOODNESS THE sun is shining," said Priscilla. "Are you sure he said he would be here sometime this morning, Mr. Johnson?"

"That's what he said," remarked the hotel manager. "Said he couldn't wait and he would hitch a lift."

"Maybe he can't get a lift," worried Priscilla. "One of us should have gone and collected him."

"And spoil the surprise? No, better this way. Dougie, the gamekeeper, is posted up on the hill and he'll wave a flag when he sees him coming."

Priscilla shook her head doubtfully, having visions of lazy Hamish stretched out asleep in the back seat of some limousine and unable to be spotted by even such an eagle eye as Dougie's. "Everything's ready anyway," she said looking around.

In the centre of the village stood a raised

platform that was normally used for school prize-giving day. Already seated on it, furtively sipping something out of a silver flask, was Maggie Baird with the shadow that was Alison beside her. Mrs. Wellington sat on Maggie's other side with her husband, the minister, and beside them were Priscilla's mother and father.

Over the street hung a banner saying, "Welcome Home, Hamish," and the school choir was lined up in front of the platform, ready to burst into song. Beside them stood the small band—one accordionist, one fiddle player, and the schoolteacher, Miss Monson, seated at the battered upright piano which was usually housed in the school hall.

Jessie and Nessie Currie, the village spinsters, were ready with *their* music, "My Heart and I." They had never been known to sing anything else.

And then from the hill above the village, Dougie frantically waved his huge St. Andrew's flag in the air. Maggie Baird walked to the front of the platform, stood before the microphone, and took a speech out of her capacious handbag while Mrs. Wellington obviously bristled with outrage.

The band struck up "Westering Home" and the little schoolchildren sang the words in their clear Highland voices. Ragged cheering broke out from the far end of the village.

Alison craned her head forwards and looked along the village street.

Her first sight of Hamish Macbeth sent all her rosy fantasies crashing into ruins. He was tall and thin and gangling with fiery red hair showing under his peaked cap. He looked half delighted and half embarrassed, and as he drew near the platform he actually blushed.

Hamish was trying very hard not to cry. He was making all sorts of grateful promises. No more laziness. No more lolling about. He would, in future, be hardworking and never, ever would he give the powers that be any excuse to send him away again.

He looked up at the platform and his eyes sharpened. The band and the choir had fallen silent. A large woman, a stranger to him, was giving him a speech of welcome. He studied her curiously, his eyes taking in the too-new tweeds, the heavy face, and the autocratic manner. He was forcibly reminded of a competent actress playing the part of a gentlewoman.

There was something about her that disturbed him and as she came to the end of her speech, she drooped one eyelid at him in a definite wink. In that moment, he had an odd feeling that inside that fat tweed-covered body was a slim beauty who had put on some sort of middle-aged disguise for a joke.

And then he realised he was being asked to make a speech.

He climbed up onto the platform, his eyes resting briefly on Alison Kerr and then turning to Priscilla, who had joined her parents. His face lit up and he gave Priscilla a singularly sweet smile.

He's not bad, thought Alison, not bad at all. He had, she noticed for the first time, hazel eyes fringed with thick lashes.

"Thank you all," said Hamish shyly. "You haff made me most welcome. I don't know quite what to say. Och, just thank you all from the bottom o' my heart."

Miss Monson began to play and Nessie and Jessie burst into their well-known rendering of "My Heart And I." When they had finished, Priscilla jumped to her feet. "Three cheers for Hamish," she shouted. And Hamish blushed as the cheers rang out and felt that awful lump in his throat. He wanted to get away and be by himself, but there was a welcome buffet luncheon laid out in the Lochdubh Hotel and more speeches, and so he forced himself to talk to everyone and try not to feel he did not deserve any of it.

Priscilla came up to him and kissed him lightly on the cheek. "Stick it out a bit longer, Hamish," she whispered. "It'll soon be over and then you can go home." Hamish looked at her with quick gratitude and then found he was beginning to enjoy himself.

"Well, copper," said a throaty voice, "aren't you going to thank me?"

He looked down at Maggie Baird. He gave her a puzzled look and then his eyes began to dance with mischief. "Are you then the leader of the Lochdubh Mafia?" he asked. "All thae crimes had poor Sergeant MacGregor not knowing whether he was coming or going."

Maggie gave a jolly laugh. "Someone had to think of something," she said. "You were very much missed and now I have met you, I can understand why."

"You are Mrs. Baird," said Hamish. "You arrived after I left for Strathbane."

"Yes." Maggie became aware that Alison was tugging furtively at her sleeve, obviously hoping for an introduction, and she swung her great bulk a little way around so that Alison was shielded from Hamish. "I don't know if I'll stay long," went on Maggie airily, "but this little place amuses me for the moment."

"If you like peace and quiet, it'll grow on you," said Hamish amiably. "I do not think I haff been introduced to this young lady." He looked over Maggie's shoulder at Alison.

"Oh, this is my niece, Alison Kerr. She's just recovered from cancer which is why she looks a bit ratty."

Alison winced and Hamish said quickly, "You

look chust fine to me, Miss Kerr. You must still
be feeling awfy frightened. I mean, you must keep
worrying that it might come back."

"Yes," said Alison gratefully. "It's made me an
awful coward, the fear, I mean. I'm frightened of
my own shadow."

"Well, I suppose that's as good an excuse as any,"
said Maggie nastily.

"One o' my cousins had an operation for cancer,"
Hamish went on as if Maggie hadn't spoken. "He's
fine now. The fear goes away after a bit. It's a bit
like getting over the death of someone you loved."

Maggie gave a musical laugh and her blue eyes
looked flirtatiously up into Hamish's own. "Is this
evening going to turn into a therapy session, or are
you going to pay some attention to your saviour?"

"Oh, aye," said Hamish with a grin. "I'm grateful
to you, Mrs. Baird."

Maggie put her hand on his arm. "And how are
you going to show that gratitude, Officer?"

He was suddenly aware of her overpowering sex-
uality, of the expensive French perfume she wore,
of being enclosed between walls of suffocating
intimacy, and instinctively drew back. He thought,
This is what a woman must feel like when a man is
undressing her with his eyes.

He hailed the arrival of Mrs. Todd, Maggie's

housekeeper, with relief. "Good evening, Mrs. Todd," he said. "It's a while since I've seen you."

Mrs. Todd was a small, sturdy woman dressed, despite the cold evening, in a black silk gown embroidered with jet that looked like an Edwardian relic. She ignored Hamish and Maggie and said to Alison, "Are you all right, Miss Kerr? I hope the festivities aren't too much for you."

Mrs. Todd's normally hard features were softened by a maternal smile. "Thank you," said Alison in a little girl voice. "I'm feeling fine."

"I've just been up to the house and put a hot water bottle in your bed and a thermos of milk on the table," said Mrs. Todd. "You're to drink every drop of that milk, mind!"

"Yes, Mrs. Todd," said Alison meekly. Normally she was grateful for the housekeeper's maternal warmth but just at that moment, she wished Mrs. Todd would go away, that Maggie would go away, and leave her to talk to this odd policeman who was the first person who had ever guessed how she really felt.

"You wouldn't think I had good central heating," said Maggie crossly.

"There's nothing mair comforting than a nice hot water bottle," said Mrs. Todd firmly.

Maggie saw Colonel Halburton-Smythe and decided to go flirt with him to liven up the evening and try her hand with the copper later on. Alison watched her go with relief but then found that Mrs. Todd was determined to stay. Hamish talked for a little to both Alison and Mrs. Todd and then was claimed by Priscilla.

"The guests are thinning out," said Priscilla. "Not long to go, Hamish. How's Mrs. Todd enjoying her job as housekeeper?"

"She's fond of that niece, Alison," said Hamish. "I suppose she enjoys the money. Mrs. Baird is supposed to be rich. Also, it gives Mrs. Todd an interest. She hasn't done much since her husband died."

"When was that again?" asked Priscilla.

"Two years? Three? Can't quite remember myself."

"And what do you make of Mrs. Baird?"

Hamish frowned. "She makes me uneasy," he said. "She's the sort of woman who creates violence. I think she's a bad woman."

"Why, Hamish Macbeth! You old-fashioned thing!"

"No, I didnae mean scarlet woman. She's spiteful to that niece of hers. She likes to be the centre of attention. She likes excitement. I think she likes affairs and yet she's too fat to have much hope at the moment."

"I wouldn't be too sure of that," said Priscilla, watching her father's flushed and excited face as he spoke to Maggie Baird.

Maggie was enjoying herself. She was aware, out of the corner of her eye, of Mrs. Halburton-Smythe's disapproval and that gave her a feeling of elation. A jealous woman acted on Maggie's spirits like a shot of adrenaline. There was a long mirror beside her on the wall. She turned to look at herself.

Robert Burns wrote:

O wad some Pow'r the giftie gie us,
To see oursels as others see us,
It wad frae mony a blunder free us,
And foolish notion.

But Maggie Baird saw herself for the first and last time in her life as she really was and instead of freeing her from foolish notions, it set in motion a catastrophic chain of events.

To see oneself as one really is—if one is ever unlucky enough to have that experience—is quite shattering. The veil of illusions and little vanities is rudely ripped aside. Maggie saw clearly a fat tweedy woman with once beautiful eyes narrowed by fat cheeks. She saw all the pettiness and meanness of soul. She saw the iron grey hair. She looked not only her age but a good bit more. Her hand fluttered up to her cheek in a helpless motion and she turned the colour of mud. She gasped for breath and swayed and the colonel shouted with alarm and rushed to support her.

Dr. Brodie, the village doctor, came bustling up. "Pills," croaked Maggie. "Handbag."

The doctor called for a glass of water while he rummaged in Maggie's handbag, stopping for an instant to look in dazed surprise at a packet of condoms before he found the pills.

Maggie gulped down the pills and slowly her colour began to return. "I'd better phone for the ambulance," said Dr. Brodie.

"No," said Maggie weakly. "I had a bit of a shock. I thought I saw someone I knew. I'll be all right. Hate hospitals. Get me home."

The competent Mrs. Todd drove Maggie and Alison home. Maggie went straight to bed, but did not go to sleep. She lay awake a long time. She quickly forgot that insight into her soul and remembered only her physical appearance. She who had once been famous for her beauty had degenerated into a fat frump. And all because of one faithless greasy waiter. She must have been mad. She remembered looking across at Priscilla as the doctor had helped her from the room. Priscilla, tall and blond and groomed, seemed to Maggie to be everything that she herself had lost.

She struck the bedclothes with her fat fist. "I'm not finished yet," she said aloud. "Look at Joan Collins!"

The little spark that the colonel's kiss had kindled grew into a flame of ambition. She lay awake long into the night, making plans.

HAMISH WALKED SLOWLY along the waterfront with Priscilla in the direction of the police station with Towser plodding along behind. The party was over. He was deeply grateful for his welcome and yet glad he no longer had to endure any of it. He did not like being the focus of attention and shrewdly judged all the celebration of his return would be followed by a backlash, the village wondering why they had gone to such lengths to get diffident and lazy Hamish back again.

He opened the kitchen door to the police station. "You'd better take a look at your living room," said Priscilla's voice behind him. He pushed open the door of the living room and blinked at the array of flower arrangements. "It's like a funeral," he said, closing the door quickly. "I'll make us some coffee."

"It was Mrs. Bisset and Mrs. Wellington. You know they do the flowers for the church," said Priscilla, sitting down on a kitchen chair. She took off her coat and eased it onto the back of the chair. "Who on earth did Maggie Baird see at that party to give her such a shock?"

Hamish shook his head. "She was looking in the

mirror. Whoever it was certainly gave her a bad fright. Where does she come from?"

"London, I believe. We had her and that niece over for dinner. Odd woman. Quite spiteful to the niece and quite repulsive looking, but Daddy was taken with her. I gather you guessed that the sudden outburst of crime in Lochdubh was to lure you back."

"I wisnae quite sure," said Hamish with a slow smile, "until I saw the welcome I got. I was so low in spirits in Strathbane, I thought you had all forgotten about me." He put two cups and saucers on the table. "Still unmarried?" he asked casually.

"Yes, still unmarried. Still training in computers. Going to be a programmer. Think I'll make a good yuppie?"

"You look what everyone believes a female yuppie to look like," said Hamish.

"With all the yuppie-bashing around, I don't know if that's a compliment or not."

"It's a compliment. You look awfy pretty—as usual."

The last was said in a matter-of-fact way. Hamish, thought Priscilla, was no longer shy in her company.

THE FOLLOWING MORNING, before Maggie awoke, Alison went out to the garage and looked longingly at the little red Renault. In the post that morning, she had received a notification that her driving test was to be held in three weeks' time in Lochdubh. When she had first arrived, she had written off for a test, confident that her benevolent aunt would surely allow her to learn to drive. That was when Maggie had been warm and kindly.

To learn to drive had become an obsession with Alison. In her dreams at night, she soared up and down the Highland roads, competent behind the wheel.

She should move to the nearest town, she lectured herself, get a job and get a car on the pay-up. Gutless, she raged at herself. But she *was* gutless. Her growing dislike of Maggie and her longing for freedom were not strong enough to enable her to face the world on her own.

She pushed her lank hair out of her eyes and crunched across the gravel to the bungalow which every day seemed more like a prison.

It was too warm, too characterless, decorated in interior designer's brown and cream with glass-topped tables; glass dining table and glass coffee table on wrought iron legs and little glass side tables. The air always seemed to smell of window cleaner, for the efficient Mrs. Todd was always polishing and shining the glass. Despite the kindness of Mrs. Todd, the kitchen was hardly the refuge it should have been. With its looped-back red and white checked gingham curtains, red geraniums in bowls, and glittering white Formica work surfaces, it looked as sterile as a stage set.

Mrs. Todd had not yet arrived. Alison made herself a cup of coffee and tried not to want a cigarette. Then she heard Maggie lumbering down the stairs, and her thin shoulders hunched as if to ward off the verbal blows about to descend on her.

To her surprise, Maggie was dressed. Usually she spent the mornings wandering around in a nightdress and dressing gown.

"I'm leaving today," said Maggie abruptly.

Alison felt a rush of relief. Maggie was abandoning her and so she would need to make a life for herself after all.

"I want you to stay here and look after things," said Maggie. "You can type, can't you?"

Alison nodded.

"Well, on the desk in the study you'll find a pile of tapes. I've been dictating my life story. I want you to type it out. High time you earned your keep."

"If you had let me learn to drive," said Alison defensively, "I could have taken a job in the village."

"What you would have earned in the village would barely have paid for the petrol," snapped Maggie. "I'll be away a few months."

"When are you leaving?" asked Alison.

"Any moment now," said Maggie, squinting at her wrist-watch. "The man from Chisholm's is coming."

Ian Chisholm, the local garage owner, had a large antique Daimler which was usually hired only for weddings and funerals. "I'm getting him to take me down to Inverness," went on Maggie. "I'll do some shopping, have dinner, and take the sleeper."

"What are you going to do?" asked Alison, beginning to brighten. Maggie was obviously not taking her car. She always left the keys in the ignition. Now, if she would only leave those keys behind, then....

"I'm going to do a bit of work on myself," said Maggie. "I've let myself go to seed. Makes two of us, hey? Although I used to be beautiful and you quite obviously never were."

All in that moment, Alison reflected that Maggie was indeed very like her sister, Alison's late mother. Alison's mother had been a colourless woman compared to Maggie, but she would say things just as Alison was preparing to go off to a school dance like, "I've done my best, but you'll never be a beauty, dear." People always said things about words not hurting you, thought Alison miserably, but they hurt like hell, the insults pilling up until one's self-esteem begins slowly to crumble under the sheer weight of them.

She thought of Maggie's mild heart attack, if that's what it had been, the evening before. She thought of Maggie's money. She, Alison, was Maggie's only relative. Had Maggie made a will? What if Maggie should die and leave her the house and the car and the money? Alison half closed her eyes. She would redecorate the house and sweep away the brown and cream and the glass tables and make it a homey place.

"Take that silly look off your face," said Maggie. "Oh, here's Mrs. Todd. Go off and get started on those tapes, Alison. I want the whole thing typed up by the time I get back."

Alison rose and went through to the room off the sitting room which Maggie called her study. It had a workmanlike desk, an electric typewriter, and there, sure enough, were the tapes and a recorder. Alison had never seen Maggie at work. Maggie must have dictated the tapes during the nights, Alison thought, or have done them some time in the past before she came north.

She began to listen to the first tape, her eyes slowly widening in horror. It was pornography. But then Maggie's life had obviously been pornographic. The first chapter dealt with Maggie's loss of virginity. Alison did not yet know that it was mild stuff compared to what was to follow.

Then above the sound of Maggie's voice, she heard the Daimler arriving. She switched off the tapes and went outside. Only one small suitcase was being loaded into the car. Mrs. Todd was standing respectfully while Maggie rapped out last-minute instructions. "And take all my clothes from my bedroom and send them to Oxfam or the Salvation Army," Maggie was saying. "I leave it to you. And see that Alison gets on with typing out that life story of mine and doesn't moon around getting lazier and spottier."

Alison, whose clear skin was her one vanity, had found two small spots on her forehead that morning. Trust Maggie to have noticed them!

And then Maggie suddenly threw her arms around Alison and gave her a warm hug. "Look after yourself, pet," she said. "That nasty cancer isn't going to come back. Just take care of yourself." There were tears in her blue eyes.

Alison hugged her back, startled and then moved.

Maggie climbed into the old Daimler, waved her fat hand once, and the car drove off.

Alison and Mrs. Todd returned to the house and sat and talked about nothing in particular and then Alison steeled herself to go back to her typing. The sudden burst of affection she had felt for Maggie after that hug was fast evaporating, to be replaced with the calculating thought, Why, the old bag's fond of me. Will she leave me her money? Please God, she leaves me her money.

Alison was a good typist. She finished the first chapter, part of her mind noting mechanically that the writing was so bad, it would surely never get published, and the other part thinking, Did she leave the car keys, and if she did, what could I do?

At last she could not bear it any longer. She went out to the garage and looked in the window of the Renault. There were the keys. Her heart began to hammer against her ribs. She felt the crumpled piece of paper that was the notification for her driving test. But even if she learned to drive, the insurance might not cover her. Perhaps the insurance covered only Maggie's driving.

She ran back into the house and began to search through the jumble of papers in the desk drawer. There it was. She opened the form up and scanned it. The insurance would cover her.

But who would teach her to drive?

And then she thought of Hamish Macbeth.

Chapter Three

Experience is the name everyone gives to their mistakes.

—Oscar Wilde

The bell at the front door of the police station rang.

Hamish sighed and put down the book he was reading. No one in the village ever rang the front doorbell. They always came to the kitchen door. The ring at the front usually meant some sort of official visit.

He was not in uniform, but it was ten o'clock at night and he had every reason to be off duty. He paused for a moment, wondering whether to answer it. Memories of Strathbane were still sharp in his mind. What if that dreadful policewoman had decided to press charges for assault?

The bell went again. He had a superstitious feeling he should not answer it. The wind howled outside. Giving himself a shake, he went slowly to the front of the police station and opened the door.

Alison Kerr stood there, blinking up at him owlishly in the blue light from the police lamp over the door.

"Come in," said Hamish. "It's a dreadful night. What's happened?"

"Nothing," said Alison as he closed the door behind her. "I just wanted to ask you a favour."

"Then come through to the kitchen and I'll make us a cup of tea. My! You're soaked through. Give me your coat."

He helped Alison out of her wet raincoat and then ushered her into the long narrow kitchen at the back of the house.

Alison sat down at the table and took off her glasses and wiped the raindrops from them with the edge of her skirt. The kitchen was warm and cheerful and Hamish, in a checked shirt and corduroys, reassuringly nonofficial.

"Now," said Hamish, "what's all this about?"

Alison clutched the mug of tea in both hands. "Maggie's gone," she said. "She says she will be away a few months and..."—Alison braced herself for the lie to come—"she says she doesn't mind if I learn to drive and my test is in three weeks' time and there isn't an instructor in Lochdubh and I

don't know anyone and I wondered if you would...
could...possibly...and..."

She fell silent and a large tear rolled down her
nose and plopped on the table.

"You want me to teach you how to drive," said
Hamish amiably. "Och, I see no reason why not.
You do have a provisional license, do you not?"

"Yes," said Alison shakily. "I've had it quite
a long time. You see, Mr. Macbeth, I've always
wanted to drive and...and...Maggie said she
wouldn't let me touch the car but she relented just
before she left."

"Where has she gone?" asked Hamish while all
the time he was thinking, Mrs. Baird never gave
this wee lassie permission to use the car. She's
lying. But then I am not supposed to know that.

"She's gone to have herself done up," said Alison,
and then blushed furiously. "I mean, she's going to
become beautiful again, she says."

"There must be a gentleman in the picture."

"No...no...I don't think so. I think she just
decided to take herself in hand. But about the
driving. When can we start? I've only got three
weeks."

"Well, things here are awfy quiet unless someone starts inventing crimes again. What about coming around here at six tomorrow evening?"

"But it's such a long way and I can't drive," bleated Alison.

"Oh, I forgot. I'll drive out then—at six."

"Thank you," said Alison. "I'm sorry I'm so emotional about it all. But you see, it's my first step towards independence. I mean, I used to be awfully confident and brave before I got cancer."

And in that heady moment, Alison believed what she had just said, forgetting the years of rabbitlike scurrying to work as secretary to the boss of a small firm which manufactured electrical components. She had been bored out of her skull but had never had the courage to hand in her notice. The factory had been on a failing industrial estate on the outskirts of Bristol, a wasteland of crumbling buildings and old beds, tyres, armchairs, and cookers, as the townspeople used it as a dump.

Hamish watched her sympathetically, reflecting that Maggie was probably the present villain in Alison's life. Timid people always had to have a villain around to maintain some shreds of self-respect. They always thought, If he or she, the husband or mother, or whoever, weren't around, then we would become successful and bold and glamorous, and when the bullies were removed from the scene by divorce or death, the rabbits immediately set out on their quests to find replacements.

"It's so beautiful up here," Alison was saying. "I feel in my bones that I am really a Highlander."

"It's quiet for a lady like yourself used to town life," commented Hamish, pouring more tea.

"Oh, things always happen to me," said Alison airily. "Adventure seems to follow me around."

The wind tore at the house and Hamish repressed a shudder. He was already regretting his generous impulse to give Alison driving lessons. He was uneasy about the whole thing, and it was not because he knew Alison was lying.

"What's the driving test like?" asked Alison.

"Well, it's not so bad here as in the towns," said Hamish. "There are no roundabouts or traffic lights. But they're very strict for all that. I don't want to depress you, but the failure rate in the British driving test is fifty-three percent. You have to train your mind to pass as well as concentrating on your driving ability. Stop worrying too much about the test and work instead at becoming a skilled driver. At the test, before you even get in the car, before you can even slide behind the wheel, you must be able to read a car number plate at a distance of sixty-seven feet. So make sure your glasses are up to the mark. Then after your test, you will be given an oral exam on the Highway Code. Have you got a copy?"

"Oh, yes," said Alison. She sighed. "I wish I were

more experienced." She cast a sudden flirtatious look at Hamish and blushed and blew her nose on a rather grubby handkerchief to cover her confusion.

"I'd better be running you back," said Hamish.

"That's very kind of you." Alison got to her feet and gazed up adoringly into Hamish's hazel eyes, but the policeman's eyes were a polite blank and he seemed to have retreated to somewhere inside of himself. Alison felt exactly as if she had made a bold pass and been ruthlessly snubbed.

It's all the fault of that Priscilla, thought Alison, she doesn't want him for herself and yet she won't let him go. By the time Hamish drove up to the bungalow—his police Land Rover having been returned to him by Strathbane headquarters— Alison had turned Priscilla in her mind into a scheming harpy.

"Won't you come in for a cup of coffee?" she asked.

"No, I'd best be getting home," replied Hamish. "See you tomorrow."

He smiled and Alison suddenly felt elated and light-hearted.

"YOU ASKED *who* to teach ye to drive?" Mrs. Todd had been in the act of whipping up a bowl of batter when Alison told her on the following day about the proposed driving lessons. She stood with her mouth slightly open, the wire whisk poised over the bowl. No modern electrical methods for Mrs. Todd.

"I asked Hamish Macbeth and he agreed. I mean the local bobby is surely the best—"

"Him!" Mrs. Todd put down bowl and spoon. "Let me tell you that man is a womaniser. The things I've heard! He's lazy and incompetent and useless. Why, when my man died, he came around, poking his nose into everything."

"But...but...I mean, the village *loves* him," wailed Alison. "You saw the reception."

"Aye, and a waste o' time and money." Mrs. Todd was a formidable figure even in her early seventies; her hair was still brown and her back ramrod straight. Her eyes narrowed suddenly. "Are you sure Mrs. Baird gave ye permission to take that car of hers out?"

"Yes," said Alison in a shrill voice. "And now I had better get back to typing out Mrs. Baird's autobiography."

"I'd like to read that," said Mrs. Todd, momentarily diverted. "She's a fine lady and has travelled a lot."

"You can ask her for a look at it when she gets back," said Alison, wondering what on earth Mrs. Todd would think of Maggie's explicitly described sexual adventures.

But Alison did not type that day; she read and reread the Highway Code, occasionally looking up at the clock to check the time and to will it to pass more quickly.

Promptly at six o'clock, Hamish drew up in the police Land Rover. To Alison's relief, Mrs. Todd had left for the day.

Alison had already opened the garage doors. Hamish stood looking at the Renault. "It's a grand wee car," he said. "But I think before the test, we'd better let Ian down at the garage have a look at it. If there's anything at all up with your car, they won't even let you start the test. Are you ready? Get in the driving seat. You'll be starting right away."

Alison climbed in and Hamish doubled his lanky length into the passenger seat beside her.

"Now," he said, "check that your seat is the right distance from the pedals and that you don't have to stretch. And then check your driving mirrors."

Alison shuffled about, jerking the car seat up too far forward and then sending it flying too far back in her excitement. Hamish got out again and took two Learner plates out of the Land Rover and fixed them to the front and back windows of the Renault.

He climbed in again and then began to instruct Alison how to move off. "Mirror, signal, then manoeuvre," he said. "You turn your head and take a quick look back before you move off. Just imagine you're out on a busy road. Turn on the engine, put the gear into first, release the clutch slowly to the biting point, that is until you feel the car surge forward a bit, and then release the handbrake."

Alison stalled several times. How could she ever get the coordination right? Driving was an unnatural act.

"I think we'll change places for a bit," said Hamish, "and I'll take ye out on the road. Hardly anyone about at this time of night."

He patiently explained everything all over again once they were out on the road while Alison, once more in the driver's seat, prayed to the God in whom she did not believe to send her wisdom.

And then suddenly she was moving slowly along the cliff road while Hamish's patient voice told her when to change gear—and then she was driving, the headlamps cutting a magic path through the night. Hamish decided to let her drive straight along for as long as possible to give her confidence. It was too early to teach her how to reverse or park. Alison, maintaining a nervous 30 m.p.h., felt she was flying as free as the wind.

At last Hamish suggested gently that he turn the car and take her home.

To Alison, Hamish Macbeth had become a

godlike figure. She was so grateful to him and so shy of him at the same time, she could hardly stammer out an offer of coffee. But Hamish Macbeth was cautious and old-fashioned and knew enough about village gossip to realise that even in this isolated spot, someone would somehow find out he had gone into the house with Miss Alison Kerr and so he refused.

HE WAS SURPRISED the following night to find a much more confident Alison, but Alison explained she had been driving up and down the short driveway all day. And then just as she was cruising along the cliff road, the engine began to cough and then died completely. "It's Maggie, that old bitch," shouted Alison. "She's been mistreating this car for years."

"Now, now," said Hamish soothingly. "I'll just hae a look under the bonnet."

Alison waited in an agony of suspense while he raised the bonnet and examined the engine under the light of a powerful torch.

He came back shaking his head. "Ian'll need to hae a look at it," he said. "Wait here and I'll walk back and get the Land Rover and we'll tow it down to Lochdubh. Have you any money?"

"I've been collecting my dole money," said Alison, "and I've quite a bit."

"Fine. Repairs are expensive, although I'll have a word wi' Ian. He owes me a few favours."

Ian Chisholm, the garage owner-cum-repairman, was not pleased at having to work after hours, and grumbled at the filthy state of the engine. "I'll dae ma best," he said at last. "But it'll cost ye. The points need cleaning and while ye're at it, it needs a new clutch plate."

"A wee word with you, Ian," said Hamish, leading him away from Alison.

Alison waited anxiously while the two men put their heads together.

Then they shook hands and Ian came back with a false sort of smile on his monkey face. "Aye, weel, Miss Kerr, it seems it won't cost that much. Hamish'll pick up yer car the morrow."

Later that night, Hamish got out his fishing tackle and set off in the driving rain to poach a salmon, praying that the water bailiffs wouldn't catch him. The salmon was in part payment for the car repairs. He did not get home until three in the morning. He put an eighteen-pound salmon on the kitchen table and went thankfully to bed after giving Towser a good rubdown, for the dog had accompanied him on his poaching expedition.

Damn Alison Kerr, was his last waking thought, that lassie fair gives me the creeps.

*   *   *

COLONEL HALBURTON-SMYTHE RUSTLED his morning paper and looked over it at his daughter's calm face. She was reading letters that had arrived for her in that morning's post.

"Looks as if we're about to have a marriage in Lochdubh," said the colonel.

"Mmm?" said Priscilla absently.

"Yes, that *friend* of yours, that Hamish Macbeth, has been courting Mrs. Baird's niece, or we all hope that's what he's been doing. He's been up at the bungalow every night."

"Oh, yes," said Priscilla absently. "Nice for him," and she continued to read her letters.

The colonel gave her bent head a pleased smile. He had been wrong. His daughter quite obviously had no romantic interest in that lazy village copper.

What on earth is Hamish playing at? thought Priscilla furiously, he can surely do better than get tied up with that little drip. He's probably sorry for her. Typical Hamish! He'll probably end up tied down for life to some dowdy female just because he's sorry for her. She picked up her letters and walked slowly from the room. She had called at the police station several evenings in a row but Hamish had always been out.

She looked at the clock. Ten in the morning. She was due to leave for London at the week-end. She'd better find out what Hamish was thinking about, fooling around with Alison Kerr.

She drove down to the police station, but although the Land Rover was parked outside, there was no sign of Hamish. She peered in the living room window. Towser was stretched out on the sofa, his eyes closed.

Now, if I were Hamish, thought Priscilla, where would I be at this time in the morning without dog or car? She stood for a moment. Small flakes of snow were beginning to fall. Her face cleared. He was probably at the Lochdubh Hotel, mooching coffee.

And that is exactly where she did run Hamish to earth. He was sitting in the manager's office, a mug of steaming coffee in his hands.

He rose in pleased surprise as Priscilla walked in. "I thought you would be back in London," said Hamish.

"Not till the week-end," said Priscilla. "Morning, Mr. Johnson. I just wanted a quick word with Hamish."

"I've got to get back to work," said the hotel manager. "Be my guest, Miss Halburton-Smythe. Help yourself to coffee."

"No, not here," said Priscilla.

"Is it police business?" asked Hamish anxiously.

"Something like that."

They walked together to the police station, Priscilla refusing to discuss what was bothering her until they were both indoors.

"It's like this," she said, not looking at him. "I've been hearing tales that you are courting Alison Kerr."

He studied her averted face and a flash of malice appeared in his eyes. "I had tae get interested in someone sometime," he said softly.

"Just so long as you're really interested in her and not just sorry for her," said Priscilla.

"Well, that iss verra kind of you, Miss Halburton-Smythe. I am glad I haff your blessing. Alison is all for a white wedding and I suppose I'll just haff to go along with it."

Priscilla sat down at the table. Towser put his heavy head on her lap and she absent-mindedly stroked his ears.

Her face was quite expressionless. Hamish looked at her thoughtfully and remembered the days when he would have given his back teeth for some sign of jealousy from Priscilla. He was glad he was not in love with her anymore, but he valued her friendship, he told himself, and even dressed as she was that morning in tweed skirt and blouse with an old oilskin coat thrown over them, she looked very beautiful. Her bright hair almost hid her face as she bent over the dog.

He sighed and sat down at the table next to her. "I am pulling your leg, Priscilla," he said. "Alison has been getting driving lessons from me. That lassie's obsessed with driving. She eats, sleeps, and drinks driving. I'm pretty sure that aunt of hers never gave her permission to use the car, but that's her problem."

"I suppose she's an interesting girl?" remarked Priscilla slowly.

"Meaning that someone as plain as that must have something going for her? Shame on you, Priscilla."

"I didn't mean that at all," said Priscilla, raising her head at last.

"She must be in her thirties but away from the driving wheel, she's scared o' her own shadow," said Hamish. "I wish I'd never agreed to teach her. She clings to me, like a limpet, emotionally, I mean. I can feel her sticky presence even when she isn't here. She's got a crush on me...for the moment. She's a walking parasite on the perpetual lookout for a host."

"Hamish!" exclaimed Priscilla, torn between relief that he was still heart free and amazement at his unexpected cruelty.

"I sound awful, don't I? But there's something unhealthy about her. I feel like swatting her with a fly swatter. It's not that she physically clings to me—she *mentally* clings and even when she's not about, I can feel that sticky mind of hers fantasizing about me."

"Really, Hamish Macbeth, are you not getting a little bit carried away? Your vanity might be prompting you into thinking she fancies you."

"Perhaps," said Hamish with a disarming smile. "Now when I'm interested, really interested in a lassie, I wouldnae know if she had a fancy for me or not unless she threw herself into my arms."

But you are no longer interested in me, thought Priscilla, rather bleakly. Aloud, she said, "Where's Maggie Baird gone?"

"I think she's gone to get herself beautified. Think it possible?"

"Hard to imagine," said Priscilla. "Is there some fellow about? Is that what caused the attack at the party? Did she see some old lover in the crowd? There were a few guests from England at the Loch-dubh Hotel who joined in the festivities."

"I've been thinking about that," said Hamish, stretching out his long legs. "I think she saw nobody but herself."

"Oh, Hamish, no one finds their own appearance such a shock."

"Not people like you. But just imagine if she had let herself go to seed but carried around in her head the image of what she used to be like. And then suddenly she saw herself in all her glory."

"Could be. I remember a fashion buyer at a store in London saying that because most of their customers were middle-aged and plump, they decided to use plump middle-aged models. It was a disaster. The buyer said she found out that when a woman buys a gown she's seen on a young and pretty model, she sees herself a little bit as that model. Interesting psychology. I'd better be going."

"Are you driving down to London?"

"No, only to Inverness. There's too much fog on the motorways at this time of year. I get the train at eight in the morning. When is Alison's driving test?"

"Time's passed quickly. It's this Friday morning."

"Well, good luck with your pupil. Bye, Hamish. See you in the summer."

"Bye." He kissed her cheek and for a moment she felt his face, unexpectedly smooth, against her own. She gave a little ducking motion of her head and turned and left the police station.

THE DAY OF Alison's driving test dawned sunny and fair, with a white frost rapidly melting from the roads and heathland. The sea loch sparkled

a three-point turn with exact precision. She sat in the car and correctly answered all Mr. Smeedon's questions on the Highway Code. When he snapped his notebook shut and picked up his clipboard, she smiled at him, waiting for the tremendous news that she had passed.

"Well, ye've failed," said the examiner.

Alison's world came tumbling about her ears. Failure again. "What did I do wrong?" she asked in a shaky voice.

"Not allowed to tell ye," he said smugly.

"But that's not true! All that's been changed. I read in the paper that examiners—" began Alison desperately. There was a rap at the window on the driving instructor's side. Smeedon looked up and saw Hamish Macbeth.

"Good day to ye, Miss Kerr," said Smeedon, opening the door and getting out. Alison laid her head on the steering wheel and wept.

"Good morning, Mr. Smeedon," said Hamish lazily. "Spring won't be far off and the thoughts of men will turn to love. But of course in your case, they've already turned."

"Blethering idiot," snapped Smeedon, beginning to stride towards his own car. Hamish put out a long arm and held Smeedon's shoulder in a strong grip. "I'm not asking ye if Miss Kerr passed her test," said Hamish, "for you were determined to fail her before she even got behind the wheel. Whit hae ye got against the lassies? I wonder what Maisie Mac-Callum would say if she knew what you were really like?"

Smeedon looked as if he had been struck by lightning. His face took on a grey tinge. Like quite a lot of first-time philanderers, he was convinced his doings were immune from the probings of prying eyes.

"You wouldnae dare," he breathed.

"I'm a verra kindly man," said Hamish, "but I hate injustice and that Alison Kerr is a champion driver—everything exactly by the book. Now if I thought you'd failed her out o' spite, there's no knowing what I'd do. They've been complaints about ye before but always from failed drivers and it was probably put down to disappointment on their part. But what if a policeman were to add his voice to the complaints? And what if that self-same policeman were a verra moral fellow and decided Mrs. Smeedon ought to know what you were up to . . . ?"

"I passed Miss Kerr," said Smeedon desperately.

"You told her?"

"Aye, well I was thinking of something else and made a wee mistake."

"Just you stand there and write out that she's passed and that'll be an end o' the matter," said Hamish.

The examiner rapidly scribbled out a form that stated that Alison Kerr had passed her driving test. Hamish twitched it out of his fingers. "Now off with you," he said sternly.

"You'll not ... ?"

"No, I won't be saying a word to Mrs. Smeedon," said Hamish, but, as the examiner scurried to his car, he added softly, "but that complaint about you failing people out o' spite is going in just the same."

He went over to the Renault, opened the door, and slid into the passenger seat.

"Here," he said, holding out Alison's pass form, "dry your eyes wi' this."

Alison took it blindly and then blinked down at it through her thick glasses. She stared at it. Then she scrubbed her eyes under her glasses with her sopping handkerchief and looked again.

"But he said I'd failed."

"We all make mistakes," said Hamish comfortably. "He's put it right."

Alison flung her arms around him and pressed a damp kiss against his cheek. "You did this," she said in a choked voice. "You made him do it."

"Now, now," said Hamish, pulling free and

resisting a strong temptation to wipe his cheek with the back of his hand. "Never mind who did or said what. You're free to drive on your own."

Alison looked at him shyly. "It's nearly lunch time," she said, "and I booked a table for us at the hotel...you know, for a celebration lunch. My little surprise."

"That's very nice," said Hamish, "but I am on duty."

"But *Hamish*!" Alison had dreamt about this lunch since she first thought of the idea.

Hamish opened the door and got out. How sweet the air outside was! It was as if Alison had been wearing a cloying sticky perfume although she never wore scent. "Take yourself for a drive and enjoy yourself," said Hamish, bending down and looking in at her. "Oh, and get a photocopy of that form and then send it off to the DVLC and you should get your licence back through the post in a couple of weeks' time." And before Alison could say any more, Hamish closed the car door and strolled off.

It was as well for Hamish that Alison was more obsessed with driving than she was with him or she would have chased after him. She sat rather bleakly, watching him in the driving mirror. Then she looked again at that pass form and a slow glow of sheer happiness spread through her body. She was free! She could drive anywhere she liked. The sun was sparkling and the road in front of her curved along the waterfront, over a humpbacked bridge and up the hill out of Lochdubh.

She switched on the engine and moved off. A car hooted and swept past her and the driver shouted something out of the window. She slammed on the brakes and sat shaking. She had forgotten to signal. She had even forgotten to check her mirrors or look around.

She tried to move off again, but the car would not budge. She switched the engine off again and covered her face with her hands. Think! Then she slowly removed her hands from her face and looked down at the handbrake. She had forgotten to release it.

There was no Hamish beside her now to prompt her.

She squared her shoulders, switched on the engine again, moved into first gear, checked her mirrors, signalled, took a quick look over her shoulder and moved off slowly. By the time she had reached the top of the road leading out of Lochdubh, she had to pull onto the side of the road to flex her hands which had pins and needles caused by her terrified grip on the wheel.

"This will never do," she said aloud.

She started off again. The road was quiet. No cars behind her and none coming the other way. Slowly, she increased her speed until she was bowling along, her hands relaxed on the wheel, but only dimly aware of the stupendous majesty of the Sutherland mountains soaring on either side of the road. She drove on and on, down past the Kyles of Sutherland and the towns of Bonar Bridge and Ardgay and then up the famous Struie Pass—famous for being a motorist's nightmare—but Alison did not know that and put her fear down to her own inexperience. The road climbed and climbed, seeming almost perpendicular and then she was running along the pass through the top of the mountains and finally down and down the twisting hairpin bends towards the Cromarty Firth which lay sparkling and glinting in the pale sunlight.

Alison came to a roundabout. A road went on over a mile-long bridge towards Inverness. On the other side of the roundabout lay the road to Dingwall. Dingwall sounded like a smaller town and therefore one with manageable traffic. She went round the roundabout and realised as she took the Dingwall road that she had forgotten to signal. All her nervousness returned.

She parked in one of the tiny town's surprisingly many car parks, choosing a space well away from other cars and spending quite twenty minutes reversing the Renault into a space that could comfortably have held three trucks.

She carefully locked up and went down to the main street to look at the shops. She stopped by a phone box and, on impulse, went in and phoned the police station in Lochdubh. There was no reply. Then Alison noticed the light was fading fast. She had a long way to drive back. She headed back towards the car park, feeling in her pocket for the car keys.

Where the keys should have been was a large hole.

Alison stopped dead. She felt sick. She retraced her steps, scanning the ground. But Dingwall should receive an award for being the cleanest town in Britain—they *vacuum* the streets. There wasn't even a scrap of paper.

She stopped someone and asked directions to the police station.

The police station was not at all like Hamish's cosy village quarters. It was a large modern building with a plaque on the wall stating that the foundation stone had been laid by Princess Alexandria. She pushed open the door and went in.

A fey-looking girl was standing at the reception desk, chain-smoking.

"My keys," Alison blurted out. "I've lost my car keys."

"We've got them," said the girl, lighting a fresh cigarette off the stub of the old one. "Just been handed in." And then she stood looking at Alison through the curling cigarette smoke.

"Oh, that's wonderful." Alison felt limp with relief. "I'll just take them."

"You can't get them till Monday," replied the girl.

"Monday! This is Friday afternoon. Monday!"

"You see that door behind me?" The girl indicated a door behind her and a little to the right which was like a house door with a large letter box. "Well, the found stuff gets put through that letter box where it falls down to the bottom of a wire cage on the other side. The person who has the key to the door has gone off for a long week-end."

"But someone else must have the key," said Alison, her voice taking on the shrill note of the coward trying to be assertive.

"No," said the Highland maiden patiently. "Only one person has the key. You see," she went on with mad logic, "if anything goes missing, we've only the one person to blame."

Alison's lips trembled. "I want my keys."

"I'll see if the sergeant can do anything." The girl stubbed out her cigarette and disappeared. After a few moments, the sergeant came back with her. Again Alison told her story and again heard the tale of the one person with the key.

"But I live in Lochdubh. I must get home." Alison was becoming terrified. What if Maggie should phone or, even worse, turn up in person?

"Now, now, we'll do our best." He called into the back of the police station and another policeman, seemingly of more senior rank, appeared.

"Och, I think we can help you," he said, and then as Alison watched, he took off his tunic and rolled up his sleeves. The sergeant produced a wire coat hanger which he proceeded to unravel, and then both policemen began to *fish* down the letter box, rather like schoolboys fishing down a drain and with as many chuckles, and "a wee but mair tae yer right, Frank," and other jolly words of encouragement.

After half an hour—the Highland police force has endless patience—the door to the police station opened and a young man rushed in. He had hair *en brosse*, a gold earring, and a desperate expression on his face. He tried to get attention but failed because the policemen were too busy fishing.

Control yourself, said Alison's inner voice. It's not the end of the world. It's only car keys. This poor man looks as if he's here to report a murder.

Aloud, she said to the young man. "Ring the bell on the wall."

He did and the sergeant turned reluctantly from the letter box. "What do you want?"

"Can I use your toilet?" asked the young man.

"Sure. Through there."

"This is madness!" howled Alison. "Look, give me the address of whoever has the key and I will take a taxi there and pick it up."

"It's twenty miles out on the Black Isle."

"I don't care," said Alison, tears of frustration standing out in her eyes.

"Och, you English are always that impatient," said the sergeant with a grin. "But we've got things in hand. We've sent out for a magnet."

The girl of the reception and the cigarettes had returned. "A magnet!" said Alison. The girl avoided her eyes and pretended to read some papers.

Another half-hour passed by while night fell outside and Alison tried not to scream at the forces of law and order and then suddenly a cheer went up. "Got 'em!"

"There you are," said the sergeant. "There was nothing for you to get upset about, now was there?"

But ungrateful Alison simply snatched the keys out of his hand and ran out without a word of thanks.

Her face tense under the glare of the sodium

street lights, she walked back through the deserted streets to the car park. Dingwall, like most Highland towns, had closed down for the night. No one will believe this, she thought, it's cloud cuckoo land.

She got into the car, switched on the lights, and began the long drive home. Night driving was misery to Alison. Approaching headlamps seemed to draw her like a moth and she kept having to twitch the wheel nervously to make sure she kept to the correct side of the road. By the time she finally parked in Lochdubh and got out of the car, her legs were trembling and she was afraid she would fall.

She rang the police station bell but Hamish had seen her coming and was lying down behind his living room sofa, waiting for her to go away.

Sadly, Alison went home. It had been a nightmare. Driving was a nightmare. She would never get back behind the wheel again.

But no sooner had she managed to park the car neatly in the garage than she found herself already restless for a new day, a day that would contain her two favourite obsessions—driving and Hamish Macbeth.

PRISCILLA CLIMBED ABOARD the Highland Chieftain, the train which was to take her from Inverness to London. Outside the snow had begun to fall and inside, the air conditioning was blasting away. She had complained before about the freezing temperature on British Rail trains and so knew she had no chance of getting any heat. She wondered savagely if the anti-pollution campaigners had thought of doing anything about British Rail. The employees, reflected Priscilla, were so bloody rude that most people preferred to drive and pollute the air rather than go by train. It was rather like entering a Kafkaesque state where ordinary laws, rules, and courtesies did not apply. The motto of British Rail should be "Sod the Public," thought Priscilla, standing up to get down a travelling case and find an extra sweater.

She sat down again and looked out of the window and there, strolling along the platform, came Hamish Macbeth. She waved to him and he climbed aboard the train and handed her a travelling rug. "Thought you might be cold," he said.

"Oh, Hamish, how sweet of you!" Priscilla put the rug over her knees. "Did you come all this way just to see me off?"

"Och, no, I haff the police business in Inverness."

"And what police business do you have that the Inverness police cannot cope with?"

"It's a secret," said Hamish stiffly. "Have a good trip and I will be seeing you in the summer."

He turned about and marched off the train.

I've offended him, thought Priscilla miserably, of course he wouldn't come just to see me off but even if he did, I shouldn't have said so. Then she noticed the travelling rug was thickly covered in dog hairs and it also smelt of dog. Poor Towser. Priscilla stroked the blanket. I hope he doesn't miss his rug too much.

Hamish walked angrily out of the station. What on earth had made him drive all the way to Inverness just to say goodbye to Priscilla? The fact was, he suddenly thought, stopping dead in his tracks and oblivious to curious stares, he missed being in love with her. He had only been hoping to stir up a few embers. And imagine giving away poor old Towser's favourite rug.

"Better buy the smelly mongrel a new one," he said aloud, "or he'll be mad at me for weeks."

He looked down and found a small middle-aged woman looking up at him curiously.

"Can I help you, madam?" he demanded, awfully.

The woman sniffed and then said, "I'm thinking ye could do wi' a bit o' help yersel', laddie, staunin' there mumbling."

Hamish walked on, pink with irritation.

Damn all women!

Chapter Four

I'd be a butterfly; living like a rover,
Dying when fair things are fading away.

—T. H. Bayly

Spring comes late to the Highlands, turning Sutherland into a blue and misty landscape; light blue rain-washed skies, far away mountains of a darker blue, cobalt blue sea.

And always through the glory of the awakening world drove Alison Kerr, propelled by her obsession with the car. She kept away from Hamish Macbeth, being of the timid nature which prefers love long distance. It was all too easy to understand he was not interested in her when she was with him; but easy to dream that he really was in love with her after all when he was absent.

So Alison was happier than she had ever been in her life. There was the magnificent stark beauty of

Sutherland, the car, the cosy, practical mothering of Mrs. Todd, the car, Hamish Macbeth, the car, no Maggie, and the car, which she had come to regard as her own.

She privately called the car "Rover," imagining it to be like a faithful and affectionate dog.

And then as spring gave way to early summer and great splashes of bell heather coloured the mountains and the nights were long and light, those northern nights where it hardly ever gets really dark, back into this paradise came Maggie Baird, although no one, not even Alison, recognised her at first.

She was svelte and beautiful with golden hair in a soft, clever style and a wardrobe of clothes by Jean Muir. She had high cheekbones and her eyes were large and very blue. She walked into the kitchen where Alison was having coffee with Mrs. Todd and stood for a moment, relishing the dawning surprise on both faces.

"Yes, it's me," she said triumphantly, if ungrammatically.

"It can't be," breathed Alison. "I wouldn't have known you. What have you done to yourself?"

"Best health farm and best plastic surgeon," said Maggie, who had also acquired a new husky voice. "Gosh, it's good to be back in Peasantville. Take my coat, Mrs. Todd. I'm expecting four guests tomorrow so I want you to get the beds ready. Hang that coat up and come back and I'll tell you about it."

Alison looked at the beautiful Maggie in a dazed way. Maggie, she reflected, was like a highly coloured butterfly that had emerged from a chrysalis of fat. Then sharp anguish struck Alison around the region of the midriff. The car! What would happen to her driving?

"Who are these four guests?" she asked instead.

"They are four fellows I used to know," said Maggie, stretching and yawning. "I've decided the single state doesn't suit me so I went through my old lists and came up with four who are likely to propose. There's Peter Jenkins, he's an advertising executive, Crispin Witherington who owns a car salesroom in Finchley, James Frame who runs a gambling club, and that pop singer, Steel Ironside."

"I thought he was dead," said Alison.

"Who?"

"Steel Ironside. He hasn't made a record in years."

"He's alive, all right."

"And you expect one of them to propose to you just like that?"

Maggie smiled slowly while Alison studied her aunt's new face for wrinkles and couldn't find one.

"I expect all of them to propose. Oh, I don't rate my charms all that much. They all need money and whichever one marries me will get it and so I'll tell 'em. Cuts you out, of course."

"How does it cut me out?" asked Alison.

"Oh, I'd made my will out in your favour but I'll change it as soon as I've made my choice."

"How's your heart?" asked Alison and then blushed.

"Hoping I'll pop off before I change my will? Hard luck, sweetie."

Mrs. Todd came back and Maggie began to tell her briskly what to do about preparing for the guests. If only Maggie *would* drop dead, thought Alison fiercely, it would all be mine, the house and the car and Mrs. Todd.

She longed for Hamish. In fact the only thing to lighten her misery at Maggie's return was that it gave her a good excuse to visit Hamish. But, oh, that dreadfully long, long walk along the coast now that she could not use the car.

"Have you finished typing that manuscript for me?" Alison suddenly realised Maggie was speaking to her.

"Yes, it's all typed up," said Alison, quickly averting her eyes so that Maggie should not see the disgust in them. The manuscript had become increasingly pornographic as it went along. Until she had read Maggie's book, Alison, who read a great deal, had thought that she knew every sexual kink and aberration there was, but Maggie's writing had introduced her to a whole new and disgusting world of sleaze. Then Alison decided to take the plunge. Better to ask Maggie about the car, this new and relaxed Maggie, and to ask her while Mrs. Todd was present.

"I've a surprise for you, Maggie," she said in a breathless rush. "I passed my driving test while you were away." The words began to tumble out. It wasn't Mrs. Todd's fault. She, Alison, had told her that she had had Maggie's permission to use the car, but Alison knew that dear Maggie wouldn't really mind because...

Her voice trailed away before the glacial expression in Maggie's now beautiful and large blue eyes.

"That is *my* car," said Maggie, "and you are not to touch it again, d'ye hear? Now I am going down to the village to stun them all with my new appearance. I may even drop in and try my hand with that copper, and while I'm gone, I suggest you start earning your keep by helping Mrs. Todd with the preparations."

She strode out, tottering slightly on her very high heels.

A few minutes later, there came the harsh sound of revving from the garage. Alison crossed to the kitchen window and looked out.

Maggie drove out of the garage. The entrance to the bungalow garden was narrow and flanked by two gateposts. As Alison watched, Maggie scraped the car along one of the gateposts on her way out. Alison let out a whimper of pain as if the car were a pet dog which was being tormented.

Mrs. Todd's calm Scottish voice sounded behind her. "I think we'd better be getting on with our work, Miss Kerr. I do not need the help but it would be as well to keep herself happy on her first day back."

Alison moved through the housework, feeling as though she were one mass of pain. That precious car that she had polished and waxed and oiled! Tears began to run down her face. She prayed to all the gods to strike Maggie Baird down.

"Come on now, lassie," said Mrs. Todd. "If I was you, I would be getting the local papers and looking for a wee job. Take ye out o' the house until you get on your feet."

"How can I take a local job when I haven't a car?" sobbed Alison.

"If ye're that desperate," said Mrs. Todd grimly, "ye'll walk. It's only fifteen miles to the village."

But fifteen miles to town-bred Alison seemed

impossible. She had done it once to go to ask Hamish about driving lessons. But to do it every day!

IT COMES AS quite a shock to the respectable female to find that quite ordinary and decent-looking men frequent tarts. When Alison first met Maggie's four guests she was surprised to find that, with the exception of the failed pop singer, they all looked normal and ordinary. The fact that Maggie, in the old days, had been what would have been called a high flyer or good-time girl did not cut any ice with Alison. She had read Maggie's manuscript and knew what she had got up to between the sheets— or in the woods, or up against walls, or on yachts— and did not realise that Maggie's less-exotic liaisons had all been pretty normal and regular.

Crispin Witherington, the owner of the car sales room, was middle-aged, like the others. He had that glossy artificial look which comes from a lot of gin and saunas. He was slightly balding, with black restless eyes, a small button of a nose, and a prim little mouth. He was expensively if tastelessly dressed, his double-breasted blazer with some impossible crest draped across his stomach and the flowered handkerchief in his breast pocket matching his flowered tie.

James Frame, from the gambling club, was tall and willowy and rabbity looking. He had a strangulated voice and appeared to cultivate a "silly ass" manner which he fondly imagined to be upper class. He had patent leather hair and smelled strongly of expensive aftershave.

The pop singer remained frozen in the age of Sergeant Pepper. He had grey shoulder-length hair, small half-moon glasses, a denim jacket and jeans, a flowered waistcoat with watch chain, and red leather shoes. He spoke with a strong Liverpudlian accent, nasal and irritating to the ear and somehow slightly phony as if he had adopted it during the Beatles era.

Finally, the advertising man, Peter Jenkins, was tall and fair with a thin, clever, rather weak face and a drawling voice. In normal circumstances, Alison would have been impressed by him, but as it was, Maggie's bedroom antics came between her and her assessment of the four men although not one of them had featured in the memoirs.

The men all talked about their surprise at getting Maggie's invitation and how marvellous she looked, while Maggie flirted and cajoled and flattered, exuding that air of maternal warmth that she seemed able to turn on at will. They all, with the exception of Maggie who had a salad and Alison who was too distressed to feel hungry, ate their way through an enormous meal.

It was when they were sitting over coffee after dinner that Maggie casually announced that she wanted to get married again and that any husband of hers would find himself a very rich man, "and probably sooner than he thinks," said Maggie, one hand fluttering to her bosom. "Got this terrible dicky heart."

It was all very neat, thought Alison, sensing the sudden stillness in the room. Maggie had said it all. She was rich and she hadn't long to live. Then the conversation became general as the men began to reminisce about old friends and acquaintances.

Maggie was the centre of attention. She was wearing a clinging dinner gown in a soft material. It was smoky blue and she was wearing a fine sapphire and diamond necklace. The skirt of the gown was folded over so that when she sat, she revealed one long leg encased in a gossamer fine stocking. Her breasts, expertly reduced in size, were displayed to advantage by the low neck of the gown. She was playful, she was amusing, she was teasing, and she threw only a few barbed remarks in Alison's direction. But she did order Alison around. "Fetch Peter a drink," or, "Move that ashtray nearer Crispin."

But as the evening wore on, the tension in the

air grew, and the men, with the exception of Peter Jenkins, the advertising executive, began to vie for Maggie's attention. Maggie persuaded Steel to get his guitar and perform. The pop singer returned with an electric guitar. While he was singing what seemed to be a protest song, Maggie began to tear up little pieces of paper napkin and pass them around to the other three men to use as earplugs. Fortunately for Steel, he was too absorbed in his performance to notice his audience was sniggering. Alison found it all very unpleasant. Her head ached. She mourned her lost days of freedom. She hadn't been able to bear to look at the car when Maggie had brought it home, a Maggie full of stories about how Hamish Macbeth had called her "a miracle."

The guests, fortunately, were tired after their journeys and an early night was proposed. Fully dressed, Alison lay in bed, waiting until she heard the large bungalow settling into silence. Then she rose and put on her coat and went downstairs and out to the garage. She opened the small side door, switched on the light and stood looking at the little red car. There was a vicious scrape along the right side. Alison began to cry in a dreary, hopeless sort of way. She had to get away from Maggie, but how could she find the strength to make the first move?

She heard steps crunch on the gravel and

switched off the light and walked outside. A tall dark figure stood outside the house, watching her.

"Who is it?" asked Alison, her voice barely above a whisper.

"Peter Jenkins."

"What do you want?"

"Just need to get some air." He moved closer, sensing rather than seeing her distress. "You upset about something?"

"It's the car," whimpered Alison. "She scraped the car."

"Maggie did? I don't understand. Is it your car?"

"No."

There was a long silence.

Then Peter let out a faint sigh. "I don't want to go back in there yet. I may as well hear your troubles. Come and sit in *my* car and tell me all about it."

"I'll bore you," said Alison.

"More than likely. But come along anyway."

His car turned out to be the latest model of Jaguar. It was parked with the others in a bit of open space outside the gateposts. He turned on the engine and switched on the heater. "It'll get warm pretty quickly," he said. "Cigarette?"

"I can't," said Alison. "I've had cancer." She began to sob and hiccup again.

He handed her a handkerchief and waited for her

to stop, then gently urged her to tell her story. Bit by bit it all came out. "If only she would die," said Alison. "She's going to change her will as soon as she chooses one of you as a husband."

"She can't choose me," said Peter. "I don't want her."

"Why was she so sure of you, then?"

The end of Peter's cigarette glowed red in the darkness as he dragged on it. Then he said, "She's changed. I had a fling with her, oh, let me see, I'm forty-eight now, say, about twenty years ago."

"How did it start?" asked Alison, curious despite her misery. "I mean, did you just say, I will pay you 'X' amount to go to bed with me?"

"No, no, that's not how the Maggies of this world operate. We went out on dates, I fell in love, she appeared to. At first it was expensive restaurants and expensive holidays, then she needed help with her mortgage, then she needed some bills paid, then it seemed logical to besotted me to give her a weekly allowance. But on my part, it was all for love."

"And then you got wise to her?"

"Oh, no, she ditched *me*, for an Arab sheik, and left for the south of France with him. It took me a long time to get over it. There's something cruel and, well...unbalanced about her now. I couldn't

94 M. C. BEATON

believe my luck when I got her letter. I didn't know she had invited the other fellows. She used to be so funny and warm and scatty and affectionate. You couldn't help forgiving her. That's why I couldn't sleep. I've been carrying a torch for her for years. Never married. What a waste!"

But Alison couldn't imagine a loveable Maggie and thought Peter a fool.

"I wish I could speak to Hamish," she said in a small voice.

"Who's Hamish?"

"The village policeman."

"But, look here, you can't report Maggie for scraping her own car!"

"No, it's not that, it's just that Hamish seems to make things all right."

"Well, as I can't sleep, I'll take you there."

"But it's after midnight!"

"If he's a conscientious bobby, he won't mind being woken up."

"All right," said Alison shyly, suddenly elated at the idea of seeing Hamish while being accompanied by this handsome man. And Peter *did* seem handsome to Alison, who did not notice the weakness in his face, having a pretty weak character herself.

Hamish Macbeth, opening the kitchen door— Alison had quickly learned that friends and locals never used the front door—thought wearily as he looked at the two faces, God help us all if the meek do inherit the earth. He tucked his shirttail into his trousers. He had been undressing for bed when he had heard the knock at the door. "Come in," he said. "I am sure it must be something awfy important to get me out o' bed." Towser stood beside his master, blinking sleepily in the light. He let out a low growl, sensing Hamish's dislike of Alison.

"Oh, *Hamish*," Alison wailed and threw herself against his chest.

Peter noticed the way the policeman quickly put Alison away from him. Fat lot of sympathy she's going to get from him, he thought, feeling suddenly protective of Alison.

"Sit down," said Hamish, "and I'll fetch us a dram."

Hamish, when he drank, preferred warm bottled beer. His sideboard contained only a bottle of twelve-year-old malt whisky, a Christmas present he had never broached. It seemed such a waste to open it now, but hospitality was hospitality and Alison, tiresome though she might be, might cheer up with a little whisky inside her.

He went back into the kitchen, carrying bottle and glasses, and poured three measures. "Now," said Hamish, "begin at the beginning and go on to the end. I have had a visit from herself today. My! Isn't plastic surgery and bleach the wondrous thing? She was like one of thae film stars, ye know, she looked like beauty preserved rather than beauty reclaimed."

Clutching her glass, Alison told the whole dismal story, of Maggie's will, of her plans to marry, of her damaging the car, and ended up with, "I can't have any respect for her, Hamish, not after having read her book."

"What book?" asked Peter Jenkins sharply.

"She's written a book about her affairs and a nasty bit of pornography it is too," said Alison. "So what am I to do, Hamish?"

"I've told you before," said Hamish quietly. "Get away from her. You're a grown woman. You can earn your own money."

"But...but...I'm still weak and what if the cancer comes back?"

"It's got more chance of coming back if you stay on with her and keep getting yourself into a state," said Hamish.

Peter Jenkins eyed the policeman coldly. What sort of help and comfort was this? In fact, what sort of policeman was this? In Peter's mind, policemen should always be on duty and always be in uniform. Hamish was wearing a tartan shirt, an old pair of cavalry twill trousers, and had thrust his bare feet into carpet slippers. His red hair was tousled and his eyelashes were ridiculously long.

"That sort of advice," said Peter, "is very easy to dole out, but very hard to take."

"But the lassie's in such misery, anything else would be better," said Hamish patiently. "What would you suggest?"

"I would suggest, Officer, that you have a word with Mrs. Baird and tell her to be nicer to Alison."

"For heffen's sake." Hamish stifled a yawn. "If Mrs. Baird wants to play the wicked stepmother and Alison here is hellbent on playing Cinderella, I can't do anything about it."

"Come along, Alison," said Peter Jenkins sternly. "There's no point in your staying here. If you ask me, it's all a great waste of time."

"I couldnae agree wi' you more," said Hamish sweetly. His hazel eyes mocked Peter. "Och, if you ask me, this lassie's got nothing to complain about. You've got to pull yourself together, Alison, you've become a right wee moaning Minnie."

Shocked and hurt, Alison stumbled to her feet. Peter put an arm about her shoulders.

"You despicable pillock," he raged at Hamish. "Don't you see she's had more than enough to bear?"

"Aw, go and boil your heid," said Hamish with lazy insolence.

Peter almost dragged Alison from the police station. As he slammed the door behind them, Hamish leapt from his chair and stood with his ear pressed against the kitchen door. "In future, Alison," he heard Peter say firmly, "you'd be better off coming to me for help."

Hamish grinned. Well, let's hope that got Sir Galahad up on his high horse, he said to himself, nothing like a bit o' knight errantry to stiffen the weakest spine.

PERHAPS BECAUSE OF Hamish's remarks, Alison tried again on the following morning to get Maggie's permission to use the car, and the resultant row sounded around the house. If Alison wanted a car that much, she could damn well buy one, said Maggie, ending up by calling her "a useless drip."

Alison was shuffling about the garden later that day, kicking the weeds, when Crispin Witherington approached. "Couldn't help hearing the row," he said.

He was dressed in what he fondly imagined suitable gear for the Highlands—lovat green cord breeches with green socks and brogues, tweed jacket, checked shirt, and a paisley cravat held in place by a large gold horseshoe. He had a rasping, rather hectoring voice, but Alison wanted sympathy.

"I hate Maggie," she muttered.

"Oh, it's just her fun. I'll bet she's fond of you. Tell you what, I'll let you drive my roller."

"I'm only used to the small car," said Alison, looking longingly to where Crispin's white Rolls Royce was parked.

"Oh, come on, have a go."

"All right," said Alison, suddenly feeling like no end of a femme fatale. Peter had shown an interest in her and now here was Crispin.

"Better drive it out onto the road for you," said Crispin. "I'll look up the map first and pick a place to go."

"I know practically all the places 'round here," said Alison, but Crispin crackled open an ordinance survey map as if she had not spoken.

"Ah, let's try this place, Fern Bay, sounds pretty."

"I know the road there," said Alison eagerly.

"Now, then, girlie, just you drive and I'll navigate. Always go by the map, that's my motto."

Alison drove off, nervously at first but then slowly gaining confidence. But it was to be her first experience of a backseat driver, or rather, a frontseat one. "Too fast," he snapped. "Slow down a bit."

Alison dutifully slowed down to thirty miles per hour.

"We'll never get anywhere if you're going to

crawl along," he said after a few minutes. "Turn off next left."

"But that's not the road to—"

"I said, turn off," he growled.

Alison reduced speed at the turn with a great crash of gears. "No wonder Maggie won't let you drive," jeered Crispin.

She slowed the big car to a halt, switched off the engine and carefully put on the handbrake, and turned to him. Enough was enough! "Why did you want me to come out with you?" she demanded in a thin, shaky voice. "I know all the roads around here and I don't care what your map says, this is a dead end."

He let out a hearty laugh although his eyes were humourless. "You ladies are always touchy about your driving. So, I'm wrong. There! I apologise. Friends?"

"Yes," said Alison weakly.

"You see, we could be of great help to each other."

"I don't see how . . ."

"Maggie's fond of you." He took out a thin gold cigarette case and extracted a cigarette. "I know she bitches at you like hell but she must like you or she wouldn't have made out her will in your favour."

"But that was before you . . ."

"Before we all turned up? I think she's playing games. I think she don't want any of us. She's changed."

"When did you . . . erm . . . meet her?"

"Ten years ago just after my marriage broke up. She came in to buy a car, a Jag, and I ended up paying for it and when our affair broke up, she sold it and bought that heap of trash she's driving around at the moment."

"That was a very good car," said Alison furiously, "before *she* startled mangling it."

"Well, have it your way. Anyway, then she was fun. It cost me a bomb but it was a barrel of laughs while it lasted." He put a pudgy hand on Alison's knee and squeezed it. "We could get along fine, girlie. Looks to me as if you haven't had much of a life. I could show you a good time."

"I would like to go home now," said Alison, her voice coming out in a squeak.

"Not yet. It's a fine afternoon. Let's find this Fern Bay and have a few noggins."

Alison hadn't the courage to stand up to him. But he had stopped navigating and criticising her driving. Alison pulled up outside Fern Bay's one pub, which was more of a shack. It was a dingy bar ornamented with posters warning crofters of the penalties to be incurred if they did not dip their sheep, an announcement of a Girl Guide rally of a few years back, and a notice saying that drink would not be served to minors. A row of small men in cloth caps leaned over the bar.

Alison felt herself beginning to blush. There were still pubs in the Highlands where the presence of a female was frowned on and she felt this was one of them.

A juke box in the corner was grinding out a seventies pop record, the sort of music which might sound catchy to someone stoned on pot, but to the clearheaded appeared a series of rhythmic thumps overtopped by a harsh voice yelling out unintelligible sounds.

Crispin approached the bar and squeezed his way in between two of the locals. "Hey, mine host," he cried. "A little service here."

"Aye, whit dae ye want?" said the barman, wiping his hands on a greasy apron. He was a great hairy man with an untrimmed red beard.

"I'll have a scotch and water," said Crispin.

"Aye, and whit aboot yer daughter?"

"I'll have the same," said Alison.

"My *friend* will have the same," said Crispin, who wondered at the same time why barmen the length and breadth of the British Isles usually referred to his female companion as his daughter, no matter what age the lady was, not knowing his offensive manner always prompted the time-honoured insult.

They sat down at a rickety plastic table by the window with their drinks.

"This is fun," said Crispin. "I like these quaint old places. It's amazing when you look about places like this and realise that Britain still does have a peasantry."

One of the small men turned from the bar and approached their table. He went straight up to Crispin who smiled at him weakly and then before Crispin or Alison could guess what the man was about to do, he whipped off his cap and butted Crispin on the forehead.

Crispin groaned and clutched his head.

"You assaulted him!" screamed Alison. "I'll call the police."

But the word *police* seemed to have an amazingly restorative effect on Crispin. "I'm fine," he said, "Let's get out of this smelly place."

When they got outside, Alison noticed he looked white and shaken and there was a lump beginning to form on his forehead.

"I'd best get you back," said Alison. "Are you sure you're all right? I mean, I could call the police." Fern Bay was probably on Hamish's beat, thought Alison, and then remembered Hamish's cruelty of the previous evening.

"No, no, I'll be all right in a tick. That little

bastard. Did you see the way he just put his cap back on and went back to his drink as if nothing had happened?"

"It's because you're English," said Alison soothingly. "They don't like the English and I don't suppose they like being called peasants either."

Maggie was waiting for them when they got back. She was holding a pile of typed manuscript.

"I've made some changes," she said nastily to Alison, "so you better get in there and start typing."

"Alison said you were writing a book. Are we all in it?" asked Peter Jenkins.

"Wait and see," said Maggie with a husky laugh. The four men who were in the living room exchanged uneasy looks. Maggie rounded on Alison. "Well, stop standing there like a drip and get to work!"

"I'd like a word with you in private, Maggie, now!" said Peter.

"Very well. Come outside."

Alison went into the study, feeling a little glow of warmth. Peter was going to give Maggie a telling off about her harsh treatment of her. The study window overlooked the garden. Alison longed to hear what Peter was saying. She pushed open the window and listened hard.

Peter's well-modulated drawl reached her ears quite clearly.

"This advertising business of mine has been going through some hard times, Maggie," she heard him say. "But I've got some new top clients and the money will be coming through soon. If you could see your way to lending me a few thousand, I can pay you back at the end of six months and at a good rate of interest, too."

"So you want my money without having to marry me to get it?" said Maggie.

"Oh, love, come here and give me a kiss. If I thought I had a hope in hell of getting you, I wouldn't have asked..."

Alison closed the window and sat down, feeling miserable. No one loved her; Hamish was fed up with her and Peter and Crispin were only making up to her because they thought she had an in with Maggie.

The study door opened and James Frame sidled in. "I say ..." he began tentatively.

"If you've come to ask me to put in a word with Maggie, forget it!" said Alison bitterly. "She hates me and I hate her and I wish I were dead but I'd like to see her in her grave first!"

"Gosh, you are in a tizzy," said James, smoothing down his patent leather hair with a nervous hand. "I only came to ask you ... well, don't you see, it's that damn book that's worrying me. Be a good chap and tell me if she's got me in it."

Alison looked at him with loathing. She hated

them all. "You're all in it," she said spitefully, "and highly pornographic it is, too. Do be an angel and tell the rest, won't you? I'm sick of being pestered and I've got work to do."

The study door opened again and this time Maggie walked in. She stopped short at the sight of James. If Alison had listened at the window a little bit longer, she would have heard Peter defending her. That and the fact that her niece had been out driving with Crispin had put Maggie in a towering rage. The sight of James bending over Alison was the last straw.

"When you've finished typing that book," said Maggie to Alison, "you can pack your things and leave."

"But I've got nowhere to go," said Alison weakly.

"Listen, Alison," said Maggie, "you've got your health and strength so I suggest you stop sponging off me and start working for a living. That whey face of yours makes me sick. I expect you to be out by the end of the week."

"Could I have a word with you, beautiful?" oiled James.

Maggie went in for one of her lightning changes of mood. "Of course," she murmured seductively. "Come up to my bedroom."

Alison sat, numb with misery, but somewhere at the bottom of her misery was a tiny feeling of relief.

The door opened again and she heard Steel Iron-side's Liverpudlian accents. "Well, that's that. She's taken that gaming club creep up to her room. He's probably getting his leg over right now."

Alison sat, rigid and silent.

The pop singer began to pace up and down the room. He was wearing a black cotton shirt open to the waist, revealing a thick mat of grey chest hair in which nestled a large gold medallion. "God, I could do with a bit of her money," he said. "I know I've got a hit. But I need the money for a backing group and then the hire of a studio."

Alison began to cry. She had been crying such a lot lately that the tears came easily, splashing onto the typewriter.

"Hey, what's up, luv?" The pop singer sat down on a chair beside Alison and peered at her through his half-moon glasses.

"Maggie's throwing me out at the end of the w-week," hiccuped Alison.

"Haven't you any place to go?"

Alison dumbly shook her head.

"Here. Give me a piece of paper. There's these bods in a squat down in Liverpool who'll take you in. Give them this note."

"You're very kind," said Alison when she could, although she thought she would rather die than move in with a lot of Liverpudlian squatters who were probably all high on dope.

"Fact is, the four of us were talking about you this morning. Maggie's gone on so much about her bad heart, in the event of her dying soon, we was saying it might be better for one of us to marry you and then divvy up the takings."

"If Maggie died," said Alison, "I would take the money, keep it, and throw you all out. I hate Maggie and I hate you."

But he merely laughed and patted her head. "Maggie's turned out a right bitch," he said. "She's enough to turn the milk. When I think what a smasher she was, warm and beautiful. Right bloody cow she is now. Don't take it out on me. With any luck, she'll drop dead. I'll survive somehow."

"I'm sorry if I was rotten to you," said Alison, "but you all seem so mercenary. Not one of you seems to like Maggie."

"It's all very well to live in slums and eat baked beans when you're young," said Steel, half to himself, "but one day you wake up old and broke and the thought of going back and starting all over is scary. Know what I mean?"

"I'm going to have a cup of coffee," said Alison, getting to her feet. "Coming?"

"Sure. Lead the way."

Mrs. Todd was in the kitchen and looked anxiously at Alison's tearstained face. "Whit's the matter, bairnie?" she said.

Alison told her of Maggie's throwing her out.

"Maybe she's worried about something," said Mrs. Todd. "Mrs. Baird's a fine decent woman and—"

"Decent!" Alison's laugh was shrill. "I never told you, Mrs. Todd, but she was and still is a tart. You should read that book of hers. . . ."

"Don't be saying nasty things about herself," said Mrs. Todd soothingly.

"S'right, all the same," said Steel, slouching around the kitchen with his hands thrust into the pockets of his jeans. "Real old whore is our Maggie."

"I will not be having that language in my kitchen!" Mrs. Todd was quite pink with outrage. The pop singer grinned and strolled out.

"Don't worry your head at the moment," said Mrs. Todd. "I have a wee bit cottage in the village and I can put you up there until you get on your feet."

"Thank you," said Alison weakly. But inside her head another prison door seemed to slam. She only half realised that she would probably accept Mrs. Todd's invitation and therefore say goodbye to any hope of independence. "I'd better get back to work," said Alison, picking up the cup of coffee Mrs. Todd had poured for her.

The bungalow had gone suddenly quiet. In her misery, she vaguely wondered where everyone was.

She sat down at the desk and forced herself to begin typing, trying to divorce her mind from the words. She heard a noisy chattering and clattering as they all met for lunch but could not bring herself to join them. She typed steadily on.

And then in the afternoon, Maggie came in. She sat down in a chair beside the desk.

"Look here, Alison," she said in her new husky voice. "You mustn't take me too seriously these days. Fact is, my nerves are screaming and I take it out on you."

Alison sat very still, her fingers resting on the keys.

"I don't know what's up with me," Maggie went on. "Half the time I seem to hate the world and I think if I see another bowl of salad, I'll puke."

"You weren't very nice to me when you were fat either," said Alison in a low voice.

"It's your own fault. There's something kickable about that cringing air of yours, sweetie. You can stay. I wish I'd never invited this lot. But I want to get married again and all men are much the same."

"But why these four?" asked Alison, curious despite her distrust of Maggie's sudden friendliness.

"They are the ones who were actually in love with me...once," said Maggie. "I got a private detective onto them and found out they all need money. I don't rate my charms that high. Stuff Women's Lib. It's still rotten trying to get the maitre d' in a restaurant if you're a single woman. And when it comes to business, men only want to deal with men. Other women pity you if you're on your own. I like a man about the place, God knows why. Anyway, it's no use looking for romance. In a marriage it all comes down to the same thing in the end: 'Why do you keep losing my socks?' But I've never settled down long enough with any man to find out what it's all about. The minute one of them got difficult, I'd give him his marching orders. Cheer up, sweetie, you're still in my will."

"I'm not interested in your money," said Alison untruthfully.

Maggie studied her for a moment and her face softened. "I think you mean that. God! I'm a bitch. Try not to take any of my moods personally. So you'll stay?"

Alison looked up into Maggie's blue eyes and received the full force of that lady's considerable personality.

"Yes," she said weakly.

"Good girl." Maggie gave her a hug, the Maggie of old, the Maggie who had swept into the hospital, the warm, maternal Maggie.

For the rest of the day, Alison felt happier than she had since Maggie's return. Maggie's change of mood permeated the house. Tomorrow, thought Alison, I'll ask her about the car.

Peter Jenkins went out of his way to be particularly nice to Alison, and Maggie did not seem to mind.

Alison slept late and awoke to the sound of the garage doors being opened.

The car!

Maggie must be about to drive it.

All at once Alison felt she just had to ask her about that car.

She threw on a dressing gown and ran downstairs and out onto the drive. The engine was coughing and choking. Maggie did not seem to be able to start it. She walked forward and stood in front of the car just as Maggie wrenched the key once more in the ignition.

One minute Alison saw Maggie's beautiful face quite clearly through the windscreen. The next, it had vanished behind a sheet of flame.

Chapter Five

O Death, where is thy sting-a-ling-a-ling
O Grave, thy victoree?
The bells of Hell go ting-a-ling-a-ling,
For you but not for me.

—British Army song

Alison had often had that very common nightmare where one opens one's mouth to scream and no sound comes out. But the scream that was wrenched from her filled the air with dreadful sound, rushing away to the high hills, sending a taunting far-off mockery of a scream echoing back.

Peter Jenkins came running out in his dressing gown and slippers to where Alison stood with scream after scream pouring from her contorted face. He ran to the blazing car, flapping his hands ineffectually.

Steel Ironside erupted onto the scene with the

kitchen fire extinguisher which he directed at the blazing car. "Help me, you faggot!" he shouted at Peter Jenkins. He ran to the car door and wrenched it open, cursing as he did so.

He grabbed Maggie and dragged her out onto the garage floor, beating at the flames on her clothes, panting and sobbing.

Mrs. Todd drove up. Her face was as white as paper as she ran for the house. She seized the phone in the kitchen and dialled 999 and demanded the fire brigade, the ambulance, and the police.

Then she went out and struck the still-screaming Alison across the face. Alison hiccupped and then ran to Peter Jenkins who gathered her into his arms.

Mrs. Todd then crouched down by Maggie. "She's dead," said Steel in a flat voice. "Her clothes had just started to catch fire when I pulled her out. She must have had a heart attack. She killed herself. I've never known anyone to mangle a car the way she did."

Crispin and James arrived on the scene, both in pyjamas.

While Peter Jenkins, still holding Alison, explained in a hushed voice what had happened, Steel said, half to himself, "It'll take hours for anything to reach us in this wilderness." The wind of Sutherland howled across the sudden hush but far away came the sound of a siren.

It came nearer, ever nearer, until the Lochdubh Volunteer Fire Brigade rolled into the drive. Close behind came Hamish Macbeth.

"Nothing for us to do now," said the fire chief, taking off his helmet and revealing himself to be Mr. Johnson, the hotel manager. He looked at the car. Smoke was still rising from the bonnet. The front of the car was burnt black.

"Don't touch anything," said Hamish Macbeth sharply. "A forensic team will have to look at that car."

"No need for that," said Crispin, marching up in all the glory of primrose-yellow silk pyjamas. "We all know Maggie wrecked that car. Something's gone in the engine and it burst into flames and gave her a heart attack. She could have got clear if she hadn't had an attack. The doors weren't locked. You policemen always complicate matters."

"Indeed? Then I'm going to complicate them further," said Hamish quietly. "The minute the ambulance has been and gone, I'll start taking statements."

Hostile eyes looked at him. Even Alison, despite her distress, thought he was being overofficious.

Hamish went back to the Land Rover. He did not believe the car had just burst into flames through some fault. Dr. Brodie had arrived and was examining the body. Hamish called Strathbane and reported a suspected murder.

When the ambulance rolled up, Hamish said in a flat voice, "Leave the body where it is." Everyone looked at him: Alison, Mrs. Todd, the four guests, the fire brigade, the doctor, and the ambulance men.

"What's up with you, Hamish?" snapped Dr. Brodie. "It's a clear case of a heart attack. I know you've solved murders in the past, but don't let it go to your head, laddie."

"I've reported a suspected murder attempt," said Hamish. The silence that followed that statement almost hummed in the ears. Then Hamish said sharply, "Who raised the bonnet of the car?"

"Och, we only lifted it up to make sure there was no flames left underneath," said Mr. Johnson crossly.

"You shouldnae hae touched anything," said Hamish. "Mrs. Todd, I think if you take Miss Kerr and the guests into the house, I'll come with you and start taking statements. We'll need to wait until the team arrives from Strathbane."

"I'll hae a word to say to your superiors," raged Mrs. Todd. "You cannae see a straightforward death when you come across it. When my man died, you was ferreting around my cupboards looking for poison."

"Had you told me your husband drank to excess, I wouldnae have had to bother," pointed out Hamish. "I was acting under orders from the procurator fiscal." The late Mr. Todd had choked to death on his vomit and poisoning had been suspected. It had indeed turned out to be poisoning, but alcohol poisoning. Mrs. Todd always maintained her husband had died of a heart attack.

Mrs. Todd went grimly into the house and began to make preparations for a breakfast-cum-lunch while the others shuffled silently into the sitting room. "Is there a room I can use?" Hamish asked Alison.

"What? Oh, yes. The study. Through there."

"Perhaps you would like to come through first, Miss Kerr. No, there is no need for you," he said to Peter, who rose at the same time as Alison and showed every sign of accompanying her.

Hamish sat down at the desk in the study. Alison had stopped crying. She looked ill

"Just tell me what you were doing this morning," said Hamish.

"I heard the car start, or rather I heard the garage doors being opened," said Alison in a shaky voice. "She...Maggie...had been kind to me the day before, so I thought I would ask her if I could drive the car. I ran down and out and just as I got to her, the car burst into flames."

"Was there any sort of bang? Any sort of explosion?"

Alison tried to concentrate. "No," she said at last. "One minute I saw her face quite clearly through the windscreen, and then it had vanished and there was nothing but flame." She showed every sign of being about to cry again.

"Now," said Hamish quickly, "let's get to the house guests. The tall one who came down that night to the police station with ye, that's Peter Jenkins. What do you know about him?"

"He's an advertising executive in his own company," said Alison. "He knew Maggie about twenty years ago, I think, or did he say eighteen? Anyway, he was in love with her and then he got her letter. You see, she wanted to get married and so she had chosen four of her old lovers. You don't seem surprised?"

"I'm surprised at her odd way of courting but not that she had a lot of lovers. Go on."

"He told me she'd changed. He wasn't in love with her anymore although I heard..."

Alison bit her lip. She had been about to tell Hamish about overhearing Peter begging for money, but Peter had held Alison and comforted her and she felt she had to protect him.

"What were you about to say?" demanded Hamish sharply.

Alison looked mutinous. He sighed and said, "I'll return to that. Tell me about the others."

"The smallish man in the yellow pyjamas is Crispin Witherington. He owns a car salesroom in Finchley in North London. He took me out driving. He wanted me to put a good word in for him with Maggie."

"Now why would he suggest that? You said yourself Maggie hated you."

"He thought Maggie was fond of me to leave me everything in her will...." Alison looked at Hamish with dilated eyes.

"Don't be in a taking," said Hamish quickly, frightened that Alison would start another scene. "The fact the woman left you her money doesn't mean you killed her for it."

"It's not that," said Alison. "How did he know? I mean, how did he know that Maggie had left me her money? And how did Steel Ironside know?"

"Maybe she told them."

"She simply wrote to them all inviting them," said Alison, "and then she told them on the first night that whoever married her would get her money and that she had a weak heart."

"But she didn't tell them she had left it to you?"

"Not that I know of. She may have said it in her letters. She told me that when she decided on one of them, she would change her will and cut me out. Maybe they overheard that. It's very easy to hear things in this house. Oh, Hamish, only yesterday she apologised for being so rude to me and she said she wouldn't cut me out of her will. Everyone will think I did it. But it *can't* be murder."

"Maybe it isn't. Go on about Mr. Witherington."

"I don't know any more except that he was one of Maggie's old flames. She made a profession of it."

"Getting money from men?"

"Yes."

"All right. Now let's move to James Frame."

"He runs a gambling club in London. He wanted me to put in a word with Maggie as well. He seems harmless enough. I didn't have much of a chance to speak to him."

"And Steel Ironside?"

"He's a failed pop singer. He told me he needed money to get started again. He seems nice. Oh, Hamish, I've just remembered. I asked Maggie why she was sure that one of these four would want to marry her and she said she'd had a private detective to check up on them and they all need money."

"Good. I'll have a look through her papers and see if I can find the name of the detective agency. Send in your friend, Peter."

Alison was soon replaced by Peter Jenkins. Hamish

looked at him curiously. But he seemed just the same as he had done when Hamish had first met him: a pleasant, if weak, man, slightly effeminate. He looked at Hamish with dislike. "You're making a fuss over nothing," said Peter, "and causing a great deal of unnecessary distress. The sooner someone higher up arrives, the better. It's a clear case of accident."

"So you say. Let's get down to business. Full name...?"

In his slow drawling voice, Peter outlined the bare facts. He had been in love with Maggie twenty years ago and had only really fallen out of love with her when he arrived and found her changed. She had invited him for two weeks and he had taken leave from his firm. He needed a holiday and so he had decided to stay.

And all the time he was talking, Hamish was thinking, He's been carrying the torch for years for a prostitute. He must be awfully immature. I wonder how he manages to run a company.

"How did you manage to set up this company?" he asked when Peter fell silent.

"I had been working for Sandford and Jones," said Peter, naming one of the biggest advertising agencies. "I was thirty when a rich uncle died and left me quite a bit so I decided to go into business for myself. My firm is Jenkins Associates."

"Doing well?"

"Very well. We've got the Barker Baby Food account, for example."

"Barker was bought over by a Japanese company last year. Do they still retain your services?"

"Of course. Didn't I just say so?"

Hamish sat back and surveyed Peter in silence.

Peter stared at him and then suddenly shrugged and said boyishly, "I shouldn't lie. A vice of advertising men. Fact is, I had this friend working with me right from the beginning and he recently quit and took that account with him. I hope the Japanese dump him."

"And what were you doing last night and this morning?"

"I was asleep the whole time. I heard Alison scream and rushed out."

"And did you hear any explosion, any loud bang?"

"No, nothing, but there could have been one before Alison woke me with her screams. It was an accident."

"Very well, Mr. Jenkins. That will be all for now. Send in Mr. Witherington."

Crispin Witherington was very jovial and hearty. Then he obviously decided that jollity was out of place and became pompous.

He outlined the facts about his relationship

with Maggie, where he was during the night and morning—in bed—his business, and his home address in a way that led Hamish to believe he had had dealings with the police before. Then he launched into a diatribe about the pub in Fern Bay and the attack on him.

"Why didn't you report it?" asked Hamish.

"What's the point," said Crispin rudely. "You local yokels stick together."

"Don't be cheeky," said Hamish mildly. "Did you want to marry Mrs. Baird?"

"Hadn't made my mind up. I only came up for a giggle."

"And yet you asked Miss Kerr for help?"

"That sneaky little drip would say anything. Look, if it is murder, you only have to look in that direction."

"Are you saying you didn't ask Miss Kerr for help?"

"I can't remember every blasted word I've said."

"I'll be getting back to you. I'll hae a word with Mr. Frame next."

James Frame sidled in, smoothing down his already smooth hair with a nervous hand. Without prompting and with many "don't you knows" and "I says," he launched into his tale of how he had been asleep the whole time.

He had almost perfected the silly-ass manner, thought Hamish, but the man's eyes behind a glaze of helpful and innocent goodwill were hard and watchful as if a smaller, meaner man were staring from behind thick glass. When he had met Maggie, he said, oh-so-long-ago, he had been doing a bit of this and a bit of that. Money in the family, don't you know. All the while, Hamish made mental notes. Lower middle class. Accent assumed. Probably was a small-time crook.

"I believe Mrs. Baird was very expensive," said Hamish.

"She wasn't a whore," said James indignantly. "We were very much in love. Of course, a chap helps out a bit with the rent and things like that, but a chap would do that for any girl."

"What is the name of the gambling club where you work?"

"The Dinosaur in Half Moon Street. That's Mayfair."

"Yes, I know where Half Moon Street is. Do you own The Dinosaur?"

"Well, not zactly. Run it for a chap."

"And the chap's name?"

"Harry Fry."

"Champagne Harry. Out of prison is he?"

James looked sulky.

Even Hamish had heard of Harry Fry. He was a con artist. His last fling had been to ingratiate himself into the graces of a colonel who was a close friend of the royal family and who lived in a grace and favour house in Windsor, that is a rent-free house given by the Crown. The colonel had gone to the Middle East to raise money for one of his favourite charities, Save the Donkeys, and had left Harry alone in his house. Harry had sold the house for a vast sum to an Arab and had been caught just as he was about to board a plane to Brazil at London airport.

His sentence had been surprisingly lenient. He had great charm and had used it to good effect in court. He had paid back all the money he had gained for the house. Harry was reputed to be worth millions. He tricked and conned only because it was the breath of life to him.

At last Hamish sent James off and Steel Ironside took his place.

"Real name?" asked Hamish.

"Victor Plummer," said the pop singer in a sulky voice. But asked about his previous relationship with Maggie, he perked up and grew almost lyrical. He might have been describing a teenage romance: Maggie's arrival on the scene, their first meeting at a party where she had shown no interest in him, the long tours, the sleazy hotels and theatrical digs, the sudden fame, the just-as-sudden falling in love and the start of the affair with Maggie, the walks in the park, the dog they had bought, the plans they had made.

"And why did she leave you?" asked Hamish.

Steel's face darkened. "Someone else came along," he said in his flat, nasal twang.

"Another pop singer?"

"No, Sir Benjamin Silver, head of Metropolitan Foods."

"The multimillionaire?"

"Yes."

"I see."

"I didn't at the time," said Steel. "That was the thing about Maggie. She went through a mint of my money but I never thought of it as paying her. I mean, she wasn't the kind you left the money on the bedside table for. I was in love and I thought she was. I thought she would come back to me."

"Are you married?"

"Separated."

"So how could you have married Mrs. Baird?"

"I'd have got a divorce. Never got around to it before."

What a weak bunch of men, thought Hamish. He took some more notes and then braced himself to interview Mrs. Todd.

He took down Mrs. Todd's account of her arrival on the scene of Maggie's death and then began to ask questions. Why had Mrs. Todd not rushed to see if she could help instead of going straight to the house and dialling 999? What had led her to believe no one had yet dialled?

"I do not know," she said primly. "It all happened that quick. They're a useless bunch and wouldnae think o' doing anything sensible."

"Very well. Where were you last night and this morning?"

"I was at a meeting of the Women's Rural Institute at the school hall, went tae my bed, and then collected some groceries in the village and drove up here."

"Do you know where Mrs. Baird meant to go?"

"I don't know. Herself usually didn't move till the afternoon. Let me tell you this, Mr. Macbeth, you are making a lot of trouble over a mere accident. You are causing poor little Miss Kerr a lot o' strain."

Hamish ignored that and ploughed patiently on with his questions.

In the sitting room, Alison sat on the sofa with Peter Jenkins beside her. His arm was around her shoulders.

"So much for that *helpful* copper of yours,"

said Peter. "I'll have his guts for giving us all this trouble."

"He wasn't at all sympathetic," sniffed Alison. "Sitting there like the Gestapo. I don't know what's come over him."

"Power, that's what. These local hick types love a chance to push their betters around."

Alison leaned back and closed her eyes. She thought about her recent interview with Hamish. She and Hamish had been friends and yet he had asked her questions as if he had never known her. God! How she hated that study. She would have it turned into a breakfast room or a library. She hated the functional desk where she had typed so much filth.

She sat up a little, frowning.

"What's the matter?" asked Peter.

"The manuscript," said Alison. "Maggie's book. I don't remember seeing it on the desk. I'd better tell Hamish about it."

"She was in there last night," said Peter. "She probably either took it to her room or put it in one of the drawers. But tell that dreary bobby if you like."

THE FOUR GUESTS had been looking forward to the arrival of Hamish Macbeth's superior, and when he did arrive, Detective Chief Inspector Blair from

Strathbane did not let them down. It was, he said, a clear case of accident. There was no need to use a squad of policemen to comb the area for clues. The car would be towed away to Strathbane and examined there. He was sure the wiring would prove to be faulty. He was so delighted at putting Hamish down before an audience that he was even nice to Steel Ironside, despite the fact that he remembered clearly that one of the pop singer's hits in the early seventies had been "Burn the Fuzz." Mrs. Todd served him coffee with cream and some of her scones. His two detectives, Jimmy Anderson and Harry MacNab, stood respectfully behind his chair. Alison, who told him about Maggie's vicious treatment of the car, thought Blair a nice fatherly man. He was heavyset and spoke with a thick Glasgow accent and when not being nice to the company treated Hamish like a moron. And Hamish deserved it all, thought Alison fiercely. After all, Hamish was a Highlander and the Highlanders were another race entirely, sly and malicious and devious.

But as if remembering at last that he, too, was a policeman, Blair became mindful of his duties and told the four men to stay at the bungalow until the forensic report came through. In a quiet voice, Hamish told him of the missing manuscript and its contents. "Hot stuff, hey?" said Blair with a

salacious leer. "I may as well hae a gander at it. Go
and find it, Macbeth, and dae something useful fur
a change."

Hamish went off. He searched Maggie's desk and
then moved quietly upstairs to her bedroom and
went carefully through all the drawers. But there
was no sign of the manuscript and no sign either of
any report from a detective agency.

At last Blair left, and the shaken guests and Alison settled down to have lunch in the kitchen.

James looked out of the window and muttered
something and then got to his feet and went over
and stared out. "Someone had better get onto Strathbane," he said. "That local bobby's making trouble."

The others joined him at the window.

The rain had started to fall quite heavily, but
Hamish Macbeth, accompanied by a large mongrel
dog, was down on his hands and knees on the gravel
in front of the garage, slowly going over every inch
of ground.

"Oh, let him get on with it," said Peter Jenkins
impatiently. "He's better out there than in here bothering us with a lot of questions."

They all returned to the table but no one seemed
to feel much like eating and at last with a clucking
noise of impatience, Mrs. Todd removed the plates
of unfinished food.

Hamish, oblivious to the rain, slowly edged backwards over the gravel, his nose almost on the ground. Then he moved over to the narrow strip of grass that bordered the right-hand side of the drive. He worked his way along, backing towards the two gateposts.

And then at the bottom of one of the gateposts he found a blackened piece of metal. He looked at it thoughtfully and then fished in his pocket for tweezers and plastic bag and popped it in.

He worked his way forward again while Towser let out a little whimper of dismay and shook himself violently, sending out a spray of water over Hamish's back. Hamish was just about to give up his search when close by where the car had stood in the garage he found a tiny piece of charred material like felt. He put that in the bag with the metal and then decided to go and see Ian Chisholm.

"Bad business up at the bungalow," said Ian. "Mind you, that car was a wreck. I hadnae seen it since I did the last repairs but it wisnae in very good shape then and that lassie, Alison, well, herself must hae driven it thousands o' miles. I suppose it just all blew."

"Maybe," shivered Hamish, steaming gently in front of the black cylindrical wood-burning stove in a corner of the garage. "But just suppose, Ian, just suppose you wanted a car tae burst into flames, would this mean anything tae ye?" He extracted the piece of blackened metal and the little bit of cloth from the plastic bag, holding each item up by the tweezers.

Ian scratched his grey hair. "My, my, ye're after another murder," he said. "Well, let me hae a think, but it'll cost ye."

"Come on, Ian, I'm not asking a favour, I am asking ye to help the forces of law and order solve a murder."

"A murder that Blair has decided is an accident?"

"Now how did you hear that?"

"Angie Burnside, him that did the garden for Mrs. Baird from time tae time, him was up at the house for he heard the siren and went for a look-see. He was still there when Blair and two fellows come out and he hears Blair say, 'I'll hae that Macbeth's balls fur trying to call an accident murder.' "

"I forgot about Angie," said Hamish. "I'd better hae a wee word with him. Anyway, use your brain, Ian."

"I hae a Renault, same age as hers, over here," said Ian. He went over to a corner of the garage where a battered Renault with a crushed side stood. He raised the bonnet and peered at the engine. Then he called Hamish over. "Let's see that bit o' metal again," said

Ian. Hamish took it out with a pair of tweezers and held it up. "Don't touch!" he warned.

"Aye, that's a sparking plug," said Ian. "Look, it could just be done, Hamish, and here's how.

"Now, if someone removed the high-tension lead from a sparking plug, and stuck this lead onto another sparking plug and laid it on top of the engine, immediately someone tried to start the engine, a spark would ignite the fumes which could be coming from, say, a petrol-soaked mat of felt resting on the engine, and, man, you'd get a bonny fire. But it still cannae be murder."

"Why not?"

"Well, although the engine would burst into flames, herself would still hae time to open the door and get clear. She'd only get a fright."

"And if that someone knew she had a bad heart?"

"Aye, man, well in that case you'd have a murder."

Chapter Six

I am a conscientious man, when I throw rocks at
seabirds I leave no tern unstoned.

—Ogden Nash

Now, thought Hamish Macbeth, if I phone Blair as a good copper should, Blair will tell me I'm talking rubbish and then slide along to the super and put it in as his own idea. If I am as unambitious as I keep telling Priscilla I am, then why should I bother? But damn it, I *do* bother.

He went into the police station office and pulled forward the typewriter and began to type out a report. When it was finished, he drove to the hotel, and despite Mr. Johnson's caustic remarks about mooching scroungers, he ran off three copies of the report on the hotel's photocopying machine. Then he headed out towards Strathbane.

He found, as he drove into the town, that he was

experiencing a slight feeling of dread, as if he would never escape again. He was glad he had left Towser behind in Lochdubh. The poor animal would probably think he was going back to the police kennels.

He drove to the police headquarters and left three of the reports plus the plastic bag with the sparking plug and scrap of felt at the desk: one of the reports to go to Detective Chief Inspector Blair, one to Superintendent Peter Daviot, and one plus the bag to go to the forensic department. Then he went back out into the night.

He decided to celebrate with a drink before returning to Lochdubh. He cast his mind back over his busy day. He had not had anything to drink so he could indulge in a small glass of whisky without being in any danger of being over the limit.

Soon Hamish was standing at the bar of an unlovely pub called The Glen, which he had recently patrolled on his beat. It still reflected the Calvinistic days when drinking was a sin and the only point in going to a pub was to get drunk. There was a bar along the end of a small room. The floor was covered with brown linoleum. There were two tables, a battered upright piano, a juke box, and a fruit machine. The whole place smelled of beer, disinfectant, damp clothes, and unwashed bodies, the habitués of The Glen dating from the days when a bath was something you had before you went to see the doctor.

"Evening, Hamish," said the barman. It had been a source of great irritation to P.C. Mary Graham that the locals on the beat all called Hamish by his first name. "Hivnae seen yiz for a long while."

"I'm back in Lochdubh," said Hamish. "I'll hae a dram."

"This one's on the hoose," said the barman. "Ye're sore missed, Hamish. That blond scunner's aye poking her nose in here, looking for trouble."

Correctly identifying the "blond scunner" as P.C. Graham, Hamish thanked him and then turned and looked around the busy bar. Several of the locals called greetings to him and he nodded cheerfully back. The customers were not working class, rather they were underclass, the denizens of the dole world who lived from one drink to the next. The juke box fell silent. A local who rejoiced in the nickname of Smelly MacCrystal lumbered to the piano. It was rumoured he had once been a concert pianist, but Hamish took that with a pinch of salt. All the habitués of The Glen claimed to have been something important at one time, from professors of English literature to jet pilots. But when only half drunk as he was that evening, Smelly could play well and he played all the old and favourite Scottish songs.

"Come on, Hamish," shouted someone. "Gie us a song."

Hamish turned red with embarrassment. He had drunk far too much on the evening of that wonderful day when he was told he could go back home and he had celebrated in The Glen by entertaining the surprised locals to a concert. He shook his head but found himself being propelled towards the piano. He shrugged and gave in.

P.C. Mary Graham quietly pushed open the door of the pub, hoping, as usual, to catch someone breaking the law. She stood there amazed.

Hamish Macbeth was standing by the piano, his fiery hair gleaming in the harsh neon lights of the pub. He was singing "My Love Is Like a Red, Red Rose." Hamish was blessed with a good voice, that kind of voice which is often affectionately described as an Irish parlour tenor. But Mary noticed only that Hamish Macbeth was leaning on the piano, singing, and surrounded by a group of dirty drunks, and he was not in uniform.

She turned and sprinted for police headquarters. As she arrived, panting and breathless, Superintendent Peter Daviot was just coming down the stairs. Now Mary should have reported to the desk sergeant who would have taken the matter higher, but she was too desperate to get Hamish into trouble to bother about the niceties of police procedure. Daviot had been looking for Blair without success. He had Hamish's report in his briefcase. He had phoned the forensic department to learn they had not started to examine the car because Blair had told them the matter was not urgent.

He listened in amazement to Mary's story. One of his officers was howling drunk in one of Strathbane's sleaziest pubs.

"We'll use my car," said Daviot. He was always worried about the police force's public image. He prayed one of the local reporters would not decide to visit the pub before he got there, the super being rather naive about the press and not knowing that if the papers wrote stories about every roistering copper, there would be little room on their pages for anything else.

He entered the pub just as Hamish was entertaining the company with a rendering of "The Rowan Tree." Daviot stopped short, listening to the mellow voice soaring in the well-known sentimental ballad. Several of the drunks were crying.

Hamish finished his song to noisy applause and shook his head when they demanded more. Then he saw the super and walked forward with a smile which quickly faded as he saw P.C. Graham's avid face behind the super's shoulder.

"Evening, sir," said Hamish mildly. "Did you get my report?"

"Yes, thank you," said Daviot. "It should have gone to Blair, you know."

"I sent him a copy as well," said Hamish. "How did you know I was here?"

"P.C. Graham was most concerned about your behaviour. She said you were drunk."

"I wonder why," said Hamish pleasantly.

"I suppose because you are not in uniform and singing in a low pub."

"This pub," said Hamish firmly, "was on my beat. You are very concerned with police image, sir, and I think you will agree that if you get along with the local community, then people are more likely to come to you in time of need."

"Just so," said the super. "Just what I always say."

"You will also agree that it iss verra important to get the facts right before troubling anyone. P.C. Graham should hae asked me a few questions. That way, she would hae found there iss no reason for me to wear uniform when off duty and that I wass not drunk."

"You mean, she did not speak to you?"

"Not a word."

Daviot swung round. "Get back to your beat, Officer," he said sternly to P.C. Graham, "and then come and see me tomorrow."

"Aye, that's right," said one of the locals, peering over the super's arm. "Tell Typhoid Mary to get the hell oot."

P.C. Graham threw Hamish a venomous look before she left.

"Come out to the car, Hamish," said the super. "I can't talk in here."

Hamish waved goodbye and followed Daviot out.

In the car, Daviot opened his briefcase and took out Hamish's report. "You say here that Mrs. Baird had employed a private detective agency to find out about these men?"

"Yes," replied Hamish, "but I couldnae find any sign of it, nor of that book she said she was writing."

"And what did Blair say to that?"

"He didnae seem interested," said Hamish, wondering at the same time why sinking the knife in Blair's fat back should make him feel so mean.

"Very well. Go back to Lochdubh and leave the matter with me. It is entirely your own fault, Hamish, that you are not in charge of this case. You have avoided promotion deliberately. I am not complaining. Good village policemen are hard to find. On the other hand, I think it is time you took a good look at yourself. You should be thinking of marriage, for example."

"I always wonder why detectives get married,"

said Hamish. "I mean, they're hardly ever home and the only friends they have outside the force are villains."

"A good, sensible wife would make allowances. It's time you settled down. I know my wife got some nonsense into her head that you might marry Priscilla Halburton-Smythe, but I said to her you would be better off with some strong village girl to look after you and iron your shirts."

"I am a dab hand wi' the iron myself," said Hamish defensively.

"Well, you'll just need to go back to your regular duties and assist the detectives when and where they need you. You are a sore disappointment to me, Macbeth."

And by that loss of his first name, Hamish knew the super was indeed angry with him.

But Daviot had given him a lot to think about. Blair would be back in Lochdubh on the morrow, throwing his weight around, and making life hell for everyone in general and Hamish Macbeth in particular. But to join the detectives, to live in Strathbane, thought Hamish as he drove slowly along the waterfront at Lochdubh. Would no one ever understand the happiness and contentment of the truly unambitious man?

Priscilla certainly did not. And there, as if his

thoughts had conjured her up, standing outside the police station under the blue lamp, was Priscilla.

He jumped down from the car. "When did you get back?"

"Today," said Priscilla. "Any chance of a cup of tea?"

Hamish led the way into the kitchen. He suddenly remembered that once when she had been in love with a yuppie called John Harrington, Priscilla had been a whole week in Lochdubh before she had thought to call on him.

John Harrington had been arrested for insider trading. Did Priscilla visit him in prison?

"See anything of that Harrington fellow?" he asked after he had made a pot of tea and they were sitting at the kitchen table.

"No, I can't. He was out on bail and he skipped the country."

"There was nothing about it in the papers," said Hamish.

"It was in the English editions. They probably didn't bother in Scotland."

The bell went at the front of the station. "Aren't you going to answer it?" asked Priscilla.

Hamish shook his head. "It'll be the press. Let them go and bother Alison. So you're up for the summer. How are things at home?"

"Not very good. Daddy's blood pressure is dangerously high. Brodie says he's got to go on a diet, but Daddy says that's a lot of rubbish. You can't tell him anything. Something's worrying him badly. Mummy says he won't talk about it and just snaps that there's nothing up."

"You look tired," said Hamish, studying her.

The beautiful oval of her face looked as flawless as ever, but her mouth drooped at the corners and her eyes were weary and sad.

Priscilla shrugged. "It wasn't a very good homecoming, which is why I am here. I felt in need of a friend. What's all this about Maggie Baird dying? Everyone thinks you a fool for saying it was murder. Tell me about it."

So Hamish did, ending up with, "Of course, it can't really be classified as murder since she died of a heart attack, so whenever we find out who rigged the car, he or she will be charged with manslaughter, but everyone knew about her weak heart, so to my mind, it's murder."

"And the obvious suspect is Alison."

"Yes, it seems as if she inherits the lot. Money's usually the root of all murders, or passion, but the guests seem a weak, mercenary lot. Maggie told them she would give her money to the one she married and that she didn't expect to live long.

Mind you, in that case, why didn't whoever wait
till she changed her will? But I can't see Alison
doing it."

"Why not?"

"That one would dream about killing Maggie,
but never actually do it. Or if by any remote chance
she did, she would use poison. It's more of a man's
murder. Crispin Witherington would know all about
car engines. I'll find out about the others."

The kitchen door opened and Alison Kerr
walked in. "Oh!" she said, looking at Priscilla in
dismay. Priscilla half rose to leave, saw the look in
Hamish's eye, and sat down again, putting an affectionate hand on Hamish's arm.

"Hamish!" said Alison, taking a chair on the
other side of Hamish and gazing into his eyes. "You
have to do something. The press keep badgering
me. They ring the bell and shout through the letter-
box. What am I to do?"

"You get Mrs. Todd to move into one of the spare
bedrooms," said Hamish wearily, "and you get her
to answer the door, and before you do that, you shut
the gates to the house and don't open them unless
you want to drive out."

"But you have to come up and tell these reporters
they are trespassing!"

"I cannae do a thing. There are no laws of

trespass in Scotland. You've got four men in the house. Can't one of them cope?"

"Peter's been marvellous. He brought me down here. He's waiting outside. He knew the press would be coming so he parked his car outside, a little down the main road. So we crept out through the garden when the press weren't looking."

"Did ye no' think of just walking through them and saying 'No comment'? Obviously not. Get Mrs. Todd. She'll handle them."

"But I can't pay her to stay all night!"

"You phone the solicitors in the morning," said Hamish patiently, "and make sure you inherit. If you do, you ask them for what money you need. You could even put a down payment on a car."

"A car! Oh, Hamish, you are clever," said Alison, throwing her arms around him, all her anger at his previous cruelty forgotten.

"Yes, yes," said Hamish testily, unwinding her arms from about his neck. "I would appreciate it, Alison, if you would phone me next time you want to come here. As you can see, I am entertaining company."

Alison blushed. Priscilla gave her a cool look and said, "Your friend must be wondering what's keeping you."

"I'm going," said Alison crossly. "You don't *own* Hamish, you know."

"My, my. Isn't money the wonderful thing," said Hamish as Alison went out, slamming the door behind her. "The worm's beginning to turn."

"I don't like that girl one bit," said Priscilla.

"Och, she's all right. She'll soon be married to another car."

Alison tried to remind herself on the road home that she should be grieving for Maggie, but she could not feel particularly sad. How much had Maggie left? Thousands! And a car! A darling little car, all her very own.

"We'll look through her papers as soon as we get back," said Peter with a smile. "I know what you're thinking about. You want a car of your own."

"Oh, Peter, you're sometimes so *perceptive*, you scare me," breathed Alison.

Alison had not searched for the will before, feeling it would be just too vulgar and insensitive. But she and Peter went straight to the study as soon as they got in and began to search through the desk. Alison was beginning to despair when Peter found it in the very front of the top drawer where it suddenly seemed to materialise in that irritating way that things do when you want them desperately—as if the household imps had got tired of the game of hide and seek and decided to let you find whatever it was you were looking for.

Alison opened it up. Her own name seemed to leap up at her and then she read on, frowning.

"What is it?" asked Peter. "Hasn't she left you anything?"

"Yes, but this is a new will. This is a copy. She must have stopped off in Inverness on her road home and made out a new one. Listen! She says that if I die, the money and the proceeds from this house and her place in London are to be divided equally among the four of you, 'the only men who ever really loved me,' that's what she says."

Peter looked at her thoughtfully. "Then you'd better just hope that one of us isn't the murderer," he said.

ALISON DID WHAT Hamish had suggested. The lawyers said their Mr. Brady was on his road to see her and she could make any arrangements with him. But, yes, they would most certainly advance her any money she wanted.

Mr. Brady arrived and read out the contents of the will to a stunned audience. For Maggie had been worth over a million pounds in investments and property. "No wonder," said Peter dryly, when the lawyer had left, "that they were so keen to lend you money."

Mrs. Todd agreed to live in. She demanded three

hundred pounds a week. Alison blinked slightly at that but readily agreed to pay her. The terror of the press receded. Mrs. Todd gave them all a piece of her mind and then firmly locked the main gates in their faces.

And while all this was going on, Hamish was dealing with a new superior. Blair had been taken off the case, although detectives MacNab and Anderson had been left on it. This detective chief inspector was called Ian Donati. His parents had come from Italy and settled in the Highlands. He was thin and sallow with clever black eyes and a lilting Highland voice. A Highland Italian, thought Hamish, thank God, having all the average Scots-man's respect for Italians.

Donati produced Hamish's report and questioned him closely. "As you seem to have a record for solving murders, I think it would be better if you accompanied us to Baird's house and sit in while we interview everyone all over again," said Donati. "Forensic men were working all night on that car to come up with the same results as your local mechanic." His manner was polite and impersonal.

Before they went into the bungalow, Anderson drew Hamish aside. "Why did ye land poor auld Blair in the shit?" he asked. "Blair's a good steady worker."

"I thought you didnae like the auld scunner!" exclaimed Hamish.

"I'd rather hae him than Donati."

Hamish grinned. "Your common nose has been put out o' joint. Donati's too classy for ye. No swearin', no slacking off, no boozing."

"Well, he shouldnae give himself airs. His folks own a restaurant in Strathbane."

"And your dad spent most of his life on the dole. You're an awfy snob, Anderson. That man's a breath o' fresh air to me. Come on."

The guests and Alison and Mrs. Todd did not like Donati. They found his quiet, dry manner and probing questions terrifying. Hamish watched and listened. Without quite saying it, Donati seemed to lay the cold facts out before the four guests: all were reported to be in need of money and were prepared to marry a woman that none of them had professed to like anymore. They all secretly blamed Alison for having dished the dirt on them to the police, not knowing it was Mrs. Todd who had told the police in no uncertain terms that she had overheard each of the men saying that Maggie had changed a lot and all for the worse.

The four men then gave their fingerprints and signed their statements and were told they could leave anytime they wanted provided they let the police know where they could be contacted. But all said they had taken leave from work and would stay. It was obvious to Hamish that Alison was to be the new target for their affections and perhaps Peter Jenkins had been clever at getting in first.

But Peter Jenkins thought that Alison might be capable of falling for, say, the pop singer and shrewdly thought that Alison clung to him because, until the reading of the will, he had been the only one to be particularly nice to her.

He was therefore relieved when Alison the next day asked him shyly if he would drive her down to the solicitors so that she could pick up a cheque from them. He readily agreed. Alison, desperate to buy a new car right away, did not even want to wait until the cheque cleared so Peter said he would put a down payment on a car for her and she could pay him as soon as she got the money. Alison spent a happy afternoon at a showroom out on Inverness's industrial estate looking at and trying out cars. To Peter's surprise, she fell in love with a bright red mini, the cheapest new car in the showroom. Made bold by Alison's timidity, he got the salesman to phone the solicitors and found to his relief that the showroom would accept Alison's cheque right away and cash it as soon as the lawyer's cheque cleared, for Peter knew he had very little left in his personal account.

That evening, it was Alison who was the centre of attention and she blossomed under it, convincing herself that her personal charms were the reason for all this sudden adoration.

And while they all fussed over Alison and paid her compliments, Donati was sitting with Hamish Macbeth in the Lochdubh police station. An effi-cient man, he had phoned Scotland Yard when he had first been put on the case, directly after Daviot returned from the pub after speaking to Hamish. He had asked Scotland Yard to phone all the pri-vate detective agencies in London. Scotland Yard had quickly found the right one and had faxed the agency's report to Strathbane.

"And here it is," said Donati, still with that pre-cise, dry manner. "I'll run through it for you. Crispin Witherington is in bad trouble. Financially, I mean. He's been in trouble in the past. He was at the centre of an investigation into stolen cars a good time ago. He was making money hand over fist. Although nothing could be proved against him, it's my guess he went straight and, not being a good car salesman or a good manager, proceeded to lose money.

"James Frame is another steady character. From research into Maggie Baird's background, it seems she often moved about that half-world of the west end of London frequented by rich criminals, drinking with the Kray brothers, that sort of thing. Oh, he knows cars. He worked, get this, at one time for Witherington. Nothing ever pinned on him. That gambling club's been raided several times for drugs but nothing ever found.

"Peter Jenkins. Good family. Educated Westminster and Christchurch, Oxford. Not a good degree. Fourth in history. Did what ex–public school boys with iffy degrees in history do—joined an advertising agency as a copy writer. Worked up to the management side. Got inheritance. Started his own firm. Did well for a bit, mainly owing to brilliant partner who recently pulled out and went into separate business and took some of the best accounts with him. Needs money or firm will fold. No money left in the family. Only child, parents dead, rich uncle was the last hope.

"Steel Ironside, née Victor Plummer, comes from village in the Cotswolds, must have adopted that accent. Sprang to fame in the late sixties during the drug culture and anti-establishment years. Was quite good-looking in a pretty, unisex sort of way, you'd never think it now to look at all that grey hair. Back in prominence in the seventies with protest songs. His hit, 'We'll Change the World,' is still sung at demonstrations but hardly by the type of people who'll pay any royalties. He wrote it. Married to some noisy slag in Liverpool. Two kids. Never sends them any money. Into drugs but who wasn't in that sort of world, nothing serious. Done a few times for carrying hash through London airport but always for himself. Never pushed or supplied. What a right lot of lulus our Maggie Baird picked."

"Who else would fall in love with a prostitute?" said Hamish primly.

Donati looked at Hamish in surprise, and then bent his head quickly to hide a smile. "Aye, maybe you're right," he said. "But the only one with a motive is Alison Kerr."

Hamish clasped his hands behind his head and stared at the ceiling. "I believe they all were in love with her at one time. She wasnae, I gather from Alison who was typing those memoirs which have mysteriously disappeared, the kind to just demand money for services rendered. It was all done under the guise of love. You know, clothes, jewels, payment disguised as presents. They're all weak men with king-sized egos. Maybe one of them nursed a lifelong grudge and wanted to get back at her. She'd developed a real bitchy manner. Could have tipped one of them over the edge. One of them could have known about the will, the new one Brady told us about. Och, but he would have to get rid of Alison."

"Exactly. I think we'd better warn her, don't you?"

ALISON WAS GETTING ready for bed when Mrs. Todd knocked at the bedroom door to say "thae polis" were back again. Alison opened the door. "Do I have to see them?" she asked weakly. She was wearing one of Maggie's white satin night-dresses with a white satin negligee trimmed with maribou. Mrs. Todd looked shocked. "I'm surprised at you, lassie. Wearing a dead woman's clothes."

"These were new," said Alison defiantly. "She'd never even taken them out of the box."

"Well, you are not seeing the polis until you make yourself look decent," said Mrs. Todd, folding her arms across her aproned bosom.

Alison wanted to scream that she was mistress of the house and would wear what she liked, but she sulkily went back into the bedroom and soon reappeared in one of her old skirts and a sweater.

"Now, that looks like my wee lassie again," said Mrs. Todd. "Come along and I'll stay with ye. It's that Macbeth that gets my back up. Too young for the National Service. He should hae been drafted as a young man. A stint in the army would hae knocked some o' the laziness oot o' him. I remember during the war when I was in the army...." But

Alison closed her ears. She was tired of Mrs. Todd's lectures. I'm fed up with her, thought Alison mutinously as she followed Mrs. Todd down the stairs, but how can I get rid of her? I know. I'll sell this place and get away from her that way.

The new millionairess walked into the sitting room and both policemen rose at her entrance.

"You may leave us," said Donati to the housekeeper.

"No, I'll stay right here," said Mrs. Todd.

"Do as you are told, woman!" snapped Donati.

"I'll be in the kitchen, Alison, if you want me," said Mrs. Todd, and Alison thought, She'll need to start calling me "Miss Kerr."

Donati said, "We have established that Mrs. Baird died because someone deliberately tampered with her car. It was manslaughter!"

Alison let out a whimpering sound. Her eyes sought those of Hamish Macbeth. Hamish stood like the epitome of the bone-headed police officer, hands behind his back, eyes on the middle distance.

"If you did not have any hand in this attempt, then we fear your life may be in danger," said Donati in that emotionless voice of his.

"Me! Why?"

"Because the four men here stand to benefit from

your death. Unless, of course, the criminal is lucky enough to get you to marry him."

Alison began to cry. Hamish reflected he had never known anyone in his life before who could cry as much as Alison Kerr.

Donati remained unmoved. "A policeman will be on constant guard at the house. Tell him if you notice anything suspicious."

Alison scrubbed her eyes. "Can I have Hamish?" she pleaded.

"No, I need Macbeth on this case and he has his village duties as well. A policeman from Strathbane will be assigned to you. Now, I am sorry to keep you further but you must tell me more about that book you were typing. Did she mention any of the four men in it?"

Alison shook her head. Hamish, glancing at her, noticed a sudden flash of alarm in Alison's eyes and wondered what she had just remembered.

"Well, I must ask you for the names of some of the men in the book. Also, did Mrs. Baird have any special friend in her heyday, I mean around about the time these four men here would have been on the scene?"

While Alison talked, Hamish found himself beginning to feel useless. Donati was asking all the questions that he, Hamish, would normally have asked behind Blair's fat back. It was very hard to feel clever and superior with Donati around. And Blair's hatred and jealousy of him, Hamish reflected, was a compliment in a way. Donati treated him as an intelligent policeman on the beat should be treated, nothing more. I'm jealous, thought Hamish ruefully.

When they had left, Alison threw herself into Mrs. Todd's sturdy arms and sobbed her heart out. "Now, then," said Mrs. Todd, "you come upstairs and I'll tuck you into bed. There, there. You poor thing. Men!"

All Alison's thoughts of asserting herself and getting rid of Mrs. Todd disappeared. It was lovely to be mothered.

But as soon as Mrs. Todd had switched out the light and left, Alison began to tremble. Which one of them would kill her for the money? Money was so important. She couldn't sleep. The wind sighed through the trees outside, a mourning sound. She shivered despite the centrally heated warmth of the room.

And then she heard a soft sound outside her door. She switched on the bedside light. The door handle began to turn. Alison opened her mouth to scream but the door opened quickly and revealed Peter Jenkins. "What do you want?" asked Alison harshly.

He came and sat on the edge of the bed and

looked down at her. "I couldn't sleep," he said. "That detective made me feel like a criminal." Peter was wearing a paisley silk dressing gown over his pyjamas and his hair was tousled. Alison found she could not feel afraid of him.

"I'm awfully scared," she said. "I can't sleep either."

He took her hand in his. "I'll sit with you for a bit."

"Thank you," said Alison shyly.

They fell silent, looking at each other. Then Peter slowly bent his head and kissed Alison gently on the mouth. She wrapped her arms around him and the next thing he was lying on the bed and a few kisses later, in the bed, and a few more and they had both managed to divest themselves of their nightwear with that strange agility of people who are determined to make love.

Their lovemaking was brief but satisfactory to both. Heaven, thought Alison just before she drifted off to sleep in Peter's arms, almost as good as driving.

Chapter Seven

*Madam, I may not call you; mistress, I am
ashamed to call you; and so I know not what to
call you; but howsoever, I thank you.*

—Queen Elizabeth I

Hamish realised on the following day that he was
letting his admiration for Donati stop him from
thinking clearly about the case. In the past, he had
relied on gossip and his own intuition. He decided
to follow his nose and go out to the bungalow and
see what he could see.

He parked his police Land Rover out on the
road. The air was clammy and still and the sea was
silent. The midges, those stinging Scottish mosqui-
toes, were out in force, and he automatically felt in
his pocket for the stick of repellent he always kept
handy.

He walked quietly up to the kitchen door and

then paused as he heard the animated sounds of conversation from within. He walked to the window and cautiously peered in. Mrs. Todd and P.C. Mary Graham were seated at the kitchen table, talking nineteen to the dozen.

He swore under his breath. He should have guessed that Strathbane would send a policewoman rather than a policeman to guard Alison.

He returned to his car and drove back down the road a little to one of those red telephone boxes you find in the isolated parts of the Highlands. This one was perched precariously on the edge of a cliff. He phoned the bungalow and, disguising his voice, asked for Alison. "Who is speaking?" demanded Mrs. Todd sharply.

"Ian Chisholm," said Hamish, and then waited.

When Alison answered the phone, he said quickly, "It's Hamish. I'm at the phone box down the road. Can you come down and meet me?"

"I can't, Hamish," said Alison airily. "I'm busy right now."

"It's very important," said Hamish. "It won't take long. And don't tell anyone where you're going."

"All right," said Alison and put down the receiver.

About ten minutes later, Hamish saw the little red mini, Alison's new pride and joy, nosing its way down the cliff road.

He waited until she had parked and then climbed into the passenger seat beside her.

"What's P.C. Graham doing inside the house?" asked Hamish. "She's supposed to be on guard outside."

"Well, she did ask for a cup of tea when she arrived but Mrs. Todd told her she was supposed to be on duty at the gate. The policewoman went off and started marching up and down like a sentry on duty. Mrs. Todd was fussing about the kitchen. She seemed edgy. She kept looking out of the window at...Mary, is it? Then she said, 'Come to think of it, I'd feel safer with her in here,' and called her in and in about a few minutes time, they seemed to be the best of friends."

"And why was that, do you think?"

"If you must know, Mrs. Todd opened the conversation by saying she was glad it was a sensible policewoman and not that idiot, Macbeth, and Mary said you were a layabout and they fell to tearing you to bits. What did you want to see me about?"

"It's about that book. When Donati asked you if there was anything about the four men in that book, you said no, but you looked startled."

"I'd just remembered something," said Alison. "I didn't want to tell Donati, because I felt like a spiteful fool. You see, I let them all think they were in it."

"Oh, my! Now about the people you remembered in the book, you said Maggie had had one friend but you couldn't quite remember the name. You said it was Glenys something."

"It's funny. I remembered during the night." Alison blushed furiously. Hamish's eyes sharpened. Alison was wearing a soft green silk blouse tucked into one of her old skirts but with a broad green leather belt with a gold clasp at her waist. She was also wearing sheer tights and high heels. She had put on eye make-up and lipstick and Hamish couldn't flatter himself all this effort was for him. So Peter Jenkins managed to score, he thought privately.

"I just remembered all at once," said Alison. "It was Glenys Evans."

"And where did she live?"

Alison shook her head.

"Anyway, I might be able to find her. Now the sooner this murderer, or would-be murderer, is caught, the better for you, Alison. I am sure all these men are rushing around you hoping to marry your fortune."

"Some of them may just like me," said Alison sharply.

"Aye, but you could talk to them and find out if any of them bore a grudge against Maggie." For the first time Hamish turned the full force of his charm on Alison. "It would be our secret."

"Oh, yes," said Alison, forgetting Peter for one glorious moment.

Hamish phoned Donati and gave him Glenys's name. But later on, his Highland curiosity got the better of him: He had an urge to talk to this woman himself. He went straight down to the post office and demanded the London telephone books. There seemed to be a great number of Evanses. He slid his thumb down the list and then stopped in surprise. For there it was in clear type, Glenys Evans, Harold Mews, London W.1.

He went back to the police station and put through a call. An autocratic voice answered the telephone and identified itself as Glenys Evans.

"It is Hamish Macbeth from Lochdubh police in Sutherland," began Hamish.

"Then you can stop right there," said Glenys. "I've already had some pig of a detective around here this morning with a most offensive manner."

Of course, thought Hamish quickly, Donati would telephone the Yard and they would have a man on the job first thing.

"I'm very sorry a lady like yourself had such a nasty experience," said Hamish. "But you see, I hae a personal interest in the matter. I wass very fond o'

Mrs. Baird and I would like to get my hands on the villain who tried to murder her."

"What! That clodhopper said she'd died of a heart attack."

"A heart attack induced by someone rigging up her car so that it burst into flames when she turned the key in the ignition. She had four guests at the house, Crispin Witherington, James Frame, Peter Jenkins, and Steel Ironside at the time, and her niece, Alison."

"I didn't know she had any relatives." There was a long silence. "All right," said Glenys at last. "If you come down here, I'll see what I can do to help."

"I don't know if that is possible," said Hamish cautiously.

"In that case, forget it."

"I'll come," said Hamish quickly. "I'll get the sleeper down tonight and be with you in the morning."

She gave him directions to her address and rang off.

If Blair had been on the case, thought Hamish, then he would just have disappeared off to London without saying anything. But Donati was a different matter.

Donati was staying at the Lochdubh Hotel. Hamish made his way there.

The detective listened to him in silence and then said colourlessly, "You stepped out of line. It is certainly unfortunate the Yard sent along someone tactless who put her back up. Do not take such actions again without my permission, do you understand?"

"Yes."

"Yes, what?"

"Yes, sir."

Hamish looked down at Donati, who was sitting in an armchair in the hotel lounge, with a tinge of surprise. "Now I suppose you'd better go. We must put personalities aside and if this woman can give you anything useful, it will be worth your fare. You may go."

And Hamish left. Blair never would have given him permission to go. Blair would have practically foamed at the mouth.

So why was it that he suddenly missed Blair?

ALISON SET ABOUT helping Hamish Macbeth. She felt she had everything in the world she had ever wanted except security. While the criminal remained at large, there was no peace, and every evening shadow held menace and every footstep on the stairs was that of an assailant. Unlike most bungalows, this one had most of the bedrooms on an upper floor with dormer windows. Peter Jenkins,

Mrs. Todd, and James Frame slept on the same floor as Alison, with Steel Ironside and Crispin Witherington in bedrooms off one of the two corridors that ran off the large sitting room. The dining room which adjoined the sitting room was little-used since Maggie's death, the guests preferring to eat their meals in the more cheerful kitchen. Another incentive to help was that despite her blossoming love for Peter Jenkins, Alison felt restless and wanted something to do to occupy her time. The efficient Mrs. Todd had made all the arrangements for Maggie's funeral and Alison had weakly left it all to her.

Alison had replied to P.C. Graham's questions about where she had been that morning by saying evasively that she had felt upset and so had gone for a little drive. Mary told her sharply not to leave the house again without saying where she was going, leaving Alison feeling more like the hired help than the lady of the house. Mrs. Todd added her own admonitions. Alison resented Mrs. Todd all over again and kept away from her as much as possible, unfairly blaming her for Mary's high and mighty manner.

Alison took pencil and paper into the dining room to start making notes on what she already had gleaned about the men's relationships with Maggie.

There was a better chance of being undisturbed in the dining room than in the study.

But no sooner had she started than Steel walked in.

"Feel like getting out of this place and going somewhere?" he asked.

Alison looked at him and thought he might still be quite presentable if he shaved and wore ordinary clothes. His shirts were always open to the waist showing that repulsive mat of hair.

"Where did you think of going?" she asked.

"Up the hill at the back. Get some fresh air."

"All right," said Alison.

To P.C. Graham's sharp question, Alison told the policewoman where they were going.

The couple walked past the garage and through a little gate in the garden fence and up a winding path that led to the top of a heathery hill behind the house. A stiff breeze had sprung up blowing warm air in from the Gulf Stream. They paused at the top of the hill and looked at the view. Great clouds were rolling in from the Atlantic and down below, the restless sea was green with flying black shadows as the clouds passed overhead.

"Can you lend me any money?" asked Steel abruptly.

"I'll need to consult my lawyers. I don't have the money yet."

"They'll advance it to you if you ask," said Steel crossly. "You've already got enough for that car of yours."

"Well, it is *my* money now."

"Look," wheedled Steel, "I've got this great song. I need money to launch it. I could pay you back with interest."

"Let me think about it," said Alison. "Isn't the view pretty?"

"Bugger the view," he said morosely.

"You must still be very upset by Maggie's death," said Alison, seizing on what she hoped was the one subject that would divert his mind from money.

"I was shocked, but not particularly upset," he said. "She'd changed. Used to be all fun and games. God! The amount of money that harpy took from me, now I think of it. At least you could say she did something for it. It's just fallen into your lap and all you do is screw around with Jenkins."

"That's not true," said Alison, her face flaming.

"Aw come *on*, you could hear the pair of you all over the house."

Alison rounded on him. "You can't have any money, not ever," she shouted.

As she ran down the hill, his jeering voice followed her, "Just mind how you go, sweetie. With you out of the way, there wouldn't be any trouble in us getting our hands on it."

Alison walked into the house. Donati was in the kitchen, telling off P.C. Graham. He had just been reminding her it was her duty to keep a watch on Alison and not to sit drinking coffee.

He subjected Alison to another long interview before taking his leave.

Alison went into the sitting room and James Frame rose at her approach. "Where's Peter?" asked Alison.

"Gone down to the village for cigarettes, I think," said James. "I've been wanting to have a talk with you."

"What about?" asked Alison, although she was sure she knew what was coming.

"Fact is, I need a bit of financial help and wondered if you could let me have a few thou'."

"No," said Alison. "Why should I?"

"Because I think you should pay me back some of the money Maggie got out of me in the past. She was insatiable. The things I had to do to find money to keep her." His voice took on a faintly cockney whine. "Come on, darling, you wouldn't miss it."

"I don't know," said Alison desperately. "Leave me alone for just now. In fact, now I think of it, I think you should all leave after the funeral. It's *my* house and I can turn you all out when I want to."

"Well, that's downright inconsiderate. I took leave and I need a holiday."

"I shouldn't think you would want to stay under the circumstances."

"I've got a strong stomach."

"I'm telling you now," said Alison as Crispin Witherington walked in. "You've all got to leave right after the funeral and that's that."

She walked back to the dining room and stood there, feeling strangely exhilarated. She couldn't remember standing up for herself before.

Then she sensed someone standing behind her and swung round. Crispin Witherington was there, a little smile curving his mouth though his eyes were hard.

"So the chips are down, are they?" he said. "No money for any of us, except perhaps what Jenkins gets for laying you. Do you know why we all rushed up here? Money. Maggie's money. Do you really think one of us gave a damn for that tart after all those years? She cheated us and conned us rotten and we all wanted some of our money back. It makes me sick to think of a wimp like you with your prissy ways walking off with that old tart's fortune. If I were you, I wouldn't walk along any dark roads for some time to come."

"Mrs. Todd!" screamed Alison.

Both Mrs. Todd and Mary Graham erupted into the room as if they had been listening outside the door.

"He threatened me," said Alison shakily. "Oh, Mrs. Todd, you've got to tell them all to go home after the funeral." And with that, Alison burst into tears, while P.C. Graham took out her notebook to question Crispin, and Mrs. Todd moved quickly forward, saying, "Come along, now. You'd best go up to your room and leave us to sort matters out here."

Alison stumbled out.

But she did not go to her room. She went out to the garage and wrenched open the doors. Driving, that was it, her only solace, her only comfort.

She roared off down the precipitous cliff road, her eyes blurred with tears. The road ran along the edge of the cliff and as Alison raced along, she realised dimly that she was going too fast to take the hairpin bends and pressed on the footbrake. Nothing happened. A corner hurtled towards her and she screeched round it and down the next stretch, her hands sweating on the wheel. Another corner was looming up. She screamed, wrenched into a low gear, and seized the handbrake and pulled with all her might. The car skidded off the road and slithered to a stop, the little front wheels of the mini hanging over the cliff edge.

Alison sat there, numb with shock. Below her the sea heaved and sucked at the base of the cliffs. She gave a whimpering sound and released her seat belt. Although she moved only slightly, the car gave a creak and seemed to dip. She twisted her neck. It was a two-door car and so she could not climb into the back seat and escape that way. It was out of the question to try to struggle through one of the back windows for they were too small and any effort to escape that way might overset the car.

She sat there for what seemed like ages while the screaming seagulls wheeled overhead. The wind was rising, she realised numbly. If she sat there much longer, one good gust would tip the little car into the sea.

Praying loudly, she grasped the door handle and pressed it down. The door swung open. Immediately below her was the sea and just behind, springy turf.

With a yell, she flung herself out of the car, twisting sideways, her fingers scrabbling at the springy turf. She lay face down, her legs dangling over the edge of the cliff. Beside her, with a sad little creak, the mini slowly slid over the edge of the cliff and plunged down into the sea.

Sobbing and grasping grass roots, Alison pulled herself forward on her belly. She heard a car drive up and a car door slam, but still she continued to ease forward until she was well clear of the cliff edge. Then she looked up.

Peter Jenkins was standing there, his hands on his hips, looking down at her.

"Whatever are you doing?" he asked. "Playing games?"

HAMISH MACBETH COULD never understand why mews cottages, those old converted carriage houses, should be considered chic. They had been built for carriages and coachmen out of the poorest of brick and usually faced north. The cobbled way outside mews cottages always seemed to be a magnet for dog owners who allowed their pets to use it as a lavatory.

The cottage owned by Glenys Evans was painted white and bedecked on the outside with honeysuckle and roses in tubs. Inside it was decorated in neo-Georgian with hunting prints on the walls, fake Chippendale furniture, and a "Persian" rug made in Belgium on the floor.

Hamish Macbeth was not a sentimental man and did not believe in the fiction of the tart with a heart and Glenys was not of the breed to prove him wrong. She was a thin, stringy woman dressed in tweed skirt, twinset, and pearls. The tarts who squandered their money went down to the gutter and the ones who invested became middle class, thought Hamish, if Glenys and Maggie were anything to go by.

Charm was not going to work with this one and so he did not waste any time in conversation but got down to the interview, asking her respectful questions and calling her ma'am.

Glenys visibly thawed before all this correct courtesy and began to talk about the old days. It was rather like listening to an opera star reminiscing about her heyday, thought Hamish. She talked of the casinos, the private planes, the best hotels, the best restaurants, her eyes filled with happy dreams. Hamish gently steered the conversation round to the four men he was interested in.

"It's all so long ago," sighed Glenys. "Let me see, Crispin Witherington." Her face darkened. "I remember *him*. Maggie and I were sharing a flat at the time. He had the nerve to say it was his flat and tried to turn us out. There was ever such a scene. But the deeds to the flat were in Maggie's name whether he paid for it or not. He was only sore because she'd ditched him for that little pipsqueak, James Frame. Now what she ever saw in him, I don't know. Anyway, I remember, she was just getting tired of him when he disappeared from the country. He wrote to say he was bankrupt, I remember. What a laugh we had about that. As Maggie said, it was nothing to do with her. He would have gone bankrupt anyway. Then Steel Ironside. I don't know that much about him. I was living in Cannes with Lord Berringsford at that time, but she was always in the papers. Said they were going to get married. Not her type. But I suppose she enjoyed all the fuss. Peter Jenkins was soppy about her. Wrote her poetry and turned white when she came into the room. She liked that. We used to have such a giggle. 'Here comes love's young dream,' I used to say. But this Arab sheik came on the scene and Maggie flipped off with him. She said he was a beast, the sheik, I mean, and she didn't get as much out of him as she had hoped.

"Wait a minute. I might have some photographs."

Hamish waited patiently while she disappeared upstairs. So much for the fallen woman of Victorian novels, he thought. Glenys showed no signs of being racked with guilt about her past. In fact, she seemed proud of it and obviously thought she had had a successful life which, indeed, in material terms, she had obviously achieved.

She came back downstairs, carrying a box of photographs which she proceeded to rummage through. "There we both are with Crispin," she said at last.

Hamish looked at the photograph. Crispin had been a fairly good-looking young man. He was standing with Maggie and Glenys beside a white Rolls Royce. Maggie was slim and blonde and Glenys a sultry brunette. They must have been a formidable pair, thought Hamish. There was a press photograph of Maggie leaving a pop concert with Steel Ironside, a thinner, younger Steel without the beard.

"What happened to her husbands?" asked Hamish suddenly.

"Baird died not long after she married him. He was a stockbroker. Taught her all about the market."

"What did he die of?"

"Heart attack. He was a lot older than her. The other one, let me see, Balfour, was a bit of a crook. Got done for doing a bank and went inside. Maggie divorced him."

"What is Balfour's first name and where did he live?"

"His name was Jimmy and he lived in Elvaston Place in Kensington, but I can't remember the number. It wouldn't help you anyway, because he rented the flat and that was years ago."

"And when did you last see Mrs. Baird?"

"The last time I saw her was about a year ago. We didn't part friends. In fact, I gave her a lecture.

Letting herself go like that and all over some two-bit waiter. 'Get on a diet,' I said. 'You look a fright, you do.' " Glenys patted her bony hips complacently. " 'You should be like me,' I said. 'You've forgotten that men are only good for one thing.' "

"Sex?"

Glenys looked amused. "No, darling, money."

"What about this waiter?" asked Hamish.

Glenys sighed impatiently and told Hamish as much as she knew about the waiter but said she could not remember either his name or where he had worked but that Maggie had allowed herself to be cheated "just like a beginner!"

Hamish asked more questions and looked at more photographs, and then finally took his leave. He felt he had learned nothing much to help towards solving the case.

He seemed to have spent hours and hours with Glenys, but he found to his surprise that it was only eleven in the morning and that he had only been with her for an hour. He decided to catch the midday train to Inverness.

During the long journey back north, he kept turning the case over and over in his head. If only Priscilla would call on him, he might be able to see things more clearly. He always did after talking to Priscilla.

But there was no one waiting for him at the police station. Only a note from Alison to say she was staying the night at Mrs. Todd's cottage in the village and would he call on her, no matter how late.

Hamish sighed. He hoped it wouldn't turn out to be a waste of time.

There was a constable on duty outside Mrs. Todd's cottage, relieving P.C. Graham. He told Hamish that Alison claimed the brakes of her car had been tampered with and that the mini had ended up in the sea after she had managed to get clear, but that a storm was blowing hard and there was no way they could get the car up until the wind died down.

Hamish knocked on the cottage door and Mrs. Todd let him in. "I told her she was safer here with me rather than staying up there with a houseful of murderers," she said, "although I don't know why she wants to see you. She's told that Italian all she knows."

Mrs. Todd led the way into her parlour. It was scrubbed and clean with comfortable old-fashioned furniture. There were several photographs of Mrs. Todd in army uniform. She must have been a holy terror, thought Hamish. Alison came down in dressing gown and slippers and Mrs. Todd went off into the kitchen to make tea.

Alison looked crushed and subdued. In a little

girl voice, she told Hamish about her escape from death, and how Steel, Crispin, and James had all tried to get money out of her. All the while, Hamish was remembering what Glenys had said. He was sure all four men had been genuinely infatuated with Maggie at one time but equally sure that they had never forgiven her for getting their money and then ditching them.

"It couldn't have been Peter, could it?" asked Alison tremulously. "I mean, he was down in the village getting cigarettes."

"It's my belief the car's brakes could have been tampered with any time. When did you last use it—I mean before you drove along the cliff?"

"The day before."

"And it was therefore just lying in the garage where anyone could get to it."

"I wish Peter were here with me," said Alison miserably.

"There's nothing to stop you from going back to your own house."

"It's not that," said Alison. "You see, I slept with him."

"So?"

Alison hung her head. "A man doesn't respect a girl for just jumping into bed with him when she hardly knows him."

"That's a pretty old-fashioned way of thinking. Last time I saw you, you looked tae me as if you'd had the experience and enjoyed every minute o' it."

"Don't!" Alison put up a hand as if to ward him off. "You men just don't understand."

Hamish sat up late that night, typing out his report for Donati. He really shouldn't be worrying so much about this case, he chided himself. Donati was highly competent. He would get Scotland Yard to ferret into all the background.

He decided to give his report to Donati first thing in the morning and then go about his village duties and only work on the case when asked to do so, and having come to that decision, he felt much better. Blair's bullying and stupidity in the past was what had spurred him on to all the effort.

He stacked the notes in a neat pile on the desk and reached over to switch off the lamp when there came a hammering at the door.

Hamish opened it. Detective Jimmy Anderson stood there, his fair hair plastered down by the rain, his face grim.

"Come along, Hamish," he said. "There's been another murder."

"Alison?"

"Naw. That pop singer, Steel Ironside."

Chapter Eight

Assassination is the extreme form of censorship.

—George Bernard Shaw

Steel Ironside lay across the bed. There was blood everywhere. The meat cleaver which had struck a deep gash right across his neck lay discarded on the floor.

Forensic men were dusting every inch of the room for fingerprints and combing the carpet for signs of clues.

Donati turned and left the room, signalling to Hamish and to the two detectives, MacNab and Anderson, to follow.

"Where are the remaining three guests?" asked Hamish. Donati paused on the stairs. "They're in the sitting room, waiting to be questioned. Mrs. Todd is on her road here with Miss Kerr."

"A meat cleaver," said MacNab. "It must hae been the Todd woman."

"As far as we know, she didn't leave Lochdubh," said Donati. "Her car engine's cold. Jenkins discovered the body. He said he was uneasy. He said he heard thumping noises coming from Ironside's room and went to investigate. He must have discovered the body minutes after the murder. The body was still warm when we got here."

He went on down the stairs and the others followed him.

The three men were grouped together in the sitting room. All looked white and strained. Crispin Witherington's eyes were blank with shock, James Frame was hugging himself and shivering, and Peter Jenkins was drinking steadily.

Donati started with Peter. "If you will just go over it again. You say you heard thumping noises. When was that?"

"I looked at my alarm clock," said Peter, "and it was just after one in the morning. I'm upstairs and Steel is...was...on the ground floor. Then I thought I heard a door slam. I decided to go down and have a look. I looked in Crispin's bedroom first. I didn't put on the light but I could make out his shape under the bedclothes in the light from the passage. Then I opened Steel's door." He gulped. "I could just make out his figure on the bed but I felt there was something wrong. I don't know why. I switched on the light and saw ... and saw ..."

"All right," said Donati. "Take it easy. Now what made you go looking after you heard ... bumps, was it? I mean, what made you think there was something up?"

"I can answer that one," said Crispin waspishly. "He thought Alison had returned and gone to bed with one of us and bang goes his millionairess."

"Is this true?" asked Donati.

"Of course it's not true," said Peter in a shrill voice. "I tell you, I can't quite explain it but there was something odd about the sounds. Then I'm sure I heard a door slam, and I wondered if Alison had changed her mind and come home."

Donati sighed. "It's a good thing the victim wasn't Miss Kerr or you all might be under suspicion. I gather from P.C. Graham that both of you, Mr. Frame and Mr. Witherington, had tried to get money out of her. If she dies, you inherit, and when we get that car of hers up, I'm sure we'll find the brakes were tampered with, that is, if this storm ever dies down."

There was a silence and all listened as the wind shrieked around the house.

The door opened and Alison came in escorted by Mrs. Todd. Alison moved like a sleepwalker.

Peter rose to meet her and held out his arms but she shrank away from him.

"Now," said Mrs. Todd, folding her arms, "which one o' ye has been using my good meat cleaver?"

Hamish had a mad desire to laugh.

"So it was your meat cleaver," said Donati. "Sit down, Mrs. Todd, and I'll get to you soon. I am going into the study and I'll interview you one by one. MacNab, you stay on duty here. Anderson, come with me and bring your notebook." He turned to Hamish and said mildly, "No need for you to stay, Macbeth. The press will be back here in droves tomorrow and they'll be at Mrs. Baird's funeral. I'll need you then."

Hamish walked out of the bungalow. Well, it was what he'd decided, wasn't it? Donati was highly competent and it was a messy murder. But as he drove back to Lochdubh, he could feel anger boiling up in him. Lochdubh was his patch. It was his responsibility to find out the murderer. He was being blinded by Donati's efficiency. Also, it was almost as if Donati had assumed the mantle of Blair and had decided he didn't want Hamish Macbeth on the case. So forget Donati and imagine the man in charge of the case to be Blair. If Blair were on the case, what then would he, Hamish, do?

Keep it very simple, he thought.

He went into the police station and made himself a cup of tea and sat down at the kitchen table. He longed for a cigarette and wondered if the longing would ever go away or whether he would be stuck with it for life.

He went through to the office and got pen and paper and then sat down at the kitchen table again and began to make notes.

He went back to the start of the case. Someone had rigged that Renault to make it burst into flames. Someone had bought a felt mat and sparking plugs. The efficient Donati had covered every garage in Sutherland. It was odd that Strathbane should have two detective chief inspectors. It meant that Donati had been recently promoted and Blair should be a very worried man for surely he was due to be demoted so that the police headquarters should have just one of them in charge. Forget Donati. Garages. There might be one somewhere else. There was a shop in Dingwall in the county of Ross and Cromarty which sold motoring accessories. Forget it. Garages and shops in the counties adjoining Sutherland had probably been covered as well. Where else?

Scrap yards. He threw down his pen. There was a sort of graveyard of old cars over at Brora. Anyone wanting cheap spare parts went there. But would four men from London know that?

He picked up the pen again and went on making notes. Gradually his head sank lower. He put his head down on the kitchen table. Just five minutes sleep, that was all . . .

HE AWOKE WITH a start. Daylight was streaming in the kitchen window. He felt stiff and grimy. He bathed and changed and shaved and went out to feed the hens. Then he got into the Land Rover and drove towards Brora. The funeral was at ten that morning. He must make sure he was back in time for it.

But when he got to the yard it was to find only a mechanic on duty who had recently started work there. The boss, he said, had taken the day off to see friends in Golspie. He'd be back that evening. Hamish stopped off at a phone box in Brora and called Priscilla.

"Look," he said urgently, "I wonder if you could do something for me. Will you be at the funeral?"

"Yes," said Priscilla. "Daddy's not going. He's getting worse. We still can't find out what's worrying him. What do you want me to do?"

"Do you still have your Polaroid?"

"Yes, it's around here somewhere."

"I want you to get photographs at the funeral of the four guests and Alison and Mrs. Todd."

"Don't be ridiculous, Hamish!" Priscilla sounded

shocked. "The press will be there in droves and if I start taking pictures as well, they'll think I'm some sort of ghoul."

"It's awfy important," pleaded Hamish. "Tell Alison and anyone else that you are taking the pictures as a memento. Tell them it's an old Highland custom. Tell them anything. Please, Priscilla."

"Oh, all right," said Priscilla crossly. "But if I get into any trouble, I'll blame you."

The wind had died down and a warm drizzle was falling as Maggie Baird's coffin was lowered into the grave. All the villagers were there as they were at any funeral in Lochdubh. It seemed to Hamish that they were nearly outnumbered by the press. Television vans stood outside the graveyard, photographers perched on the top of tombstones, and reporters in black ties stood respectfully around, although questioning everyone they could get hold of in hushed whispers.

The funeral reception was to be held in the village hall, Mrs. Todd and the minister's wife, Mrs. Wellington, having decided Alison would not be able to manage the funeral baked meats on her own. Hamish reflected that it might have been better if the organisation of the reception *had* been left to Alison. She looked very frail and she had nothing to take her mind off her fears.

Priscilla was discreetly taking photographs but there were so many press photographers around that no one seemed to notice.

At the funeral reception, she handed Hamish the photographs. "When this is all over," said Hamish, "let's you and me go off somewhere and talk. You're not looking your usual bonny self these days."

"I'm worried about Daddy," said Priscilla. "Yes, I'd like that. The atmosphere at home is all gloom and doom. Did you see Daddy at the funeral? Why on earth did he decide to come along? Thank goodness he didn't stay for the reception. There is so much whisky on offer here and Daddy's been sinking quite a lot of it recently. Look at this photograph. He's standing with Mrs. Todd and Alison. See how swollen his face is? He's all bloated up. He won't go to Dr. Brodie anymore either."

Hamish wondered whether to tell Donati where he was going. But Donati would simply phone the police at Brora and tell Hamish sharply to leave the case alone. Something made Hamish approach Donati and say earnestly, "I've got some ideas about the case I would like to put to you, sir."

Donati frowned. "I haven't time to listen to you at the moment," he said. "The press are all over the place. The wind has died down so we've got a chance of getting that car up out of the sea.

Just stand by for the moment until I give you your orders."

Hamish humbly touched his cap and strolled away. He obeyed orders for the rest of the day and even the news that he was to guard the bungalow from the press in the company of P.C. Graham didn't seem to ruffle him. He stood by one gate-post and P.C. Graham stood at the other, flashing him an occasional venomous glance. At six o'clock, Hamish looked at his watch and then began to walk off down the drive.

"Hey, you!" yelled Mary Graham. "Where dae ye think you're going?"

But Hamish did not even turn around.

As he was driving along the waterfront, he saw the gnarled figure of the gardener, Angus Burnside, leaning over the sea wall and drew up.

Angus turned round. "Ach, what is it noo, Hamish?" he asked crossly. "I've been answering the polis's questions fur days."

"Well, humour me, Angie," said Hamish. "When you were working around that bungalow, did you see anyone go into that garage apart from Miss Kerr and Mrs. Baird?"

"That wee greaser wi' the uppity manner."

"Which could apply to all of them," said Hamish patiently. "Which one was it?"

"The smarmy one, him called Witherington. It wass about twa days afore the death o' Mrs. Baird. 'Whit d'ye want?' I went and asked him, and he got very hoity-toity. 'Go back to your gardening, my good fellow,' he says. Damp English. They should all stay on the other side o' the border."

"Anyone else apart from him?"

"Naw, no one but that daftie, Miss Kerr. D'ye ken, she used tae go and *talk* tae that car!"

Hamish thanked him and drove off on the long road to Brora again. It was still high summer and in the north of Scotland it hardly ever gets dark. There was a blazing sunset as he arrived at the scrap yard. The derelict cars lay about in various stages of rust and decay. The purple flowers of the willow herb bloomed amongst the heaps of twentieth-century junk and long sour grass sprouted through shattered doors and windows of the less popular models—less popular for their spare parts. The whole thing was like a graveyard, a monument, a tombstone to death on the roads. That Ford over there, thought Hamish, had anyone survived that crash? The whole front was smashed and buckled.

Somewhere a dog howled dismally and the wind whistled through the rusty cars and swaying grass. At least the rain has stopped, thought Hamish, picking his way round the muddy puddles to a hut in the middle of the yard.

Cars, he thought. This case is all about cars. Forget the meat cleaver for the moment. Cars. Crispin knew about cars. James Frame once worked for him. The others probably knew a bit about car engines. Alison's obsession with driving. What an odd girl she was. Pity she seemed to have taken an aversion to Jenkins. A weak man to look after was just what she needed to stiffen her spine.

There was no one in the hut. Hamish sighed impatiently and sat down in a battered armchair beside the hut door to wait. He was very tired. Poor Priscilla. What on earth could be bothering that father of hers? He couldn't help there. The colonel loathed him. His eyes began to close. Then he heard the sound of a car approaching and straightened up.

The owner of the scrap yard, a small greying man in blue overalls, drove up.

"What do ye want?" he demanded as he approached Hamish. "There's not one stolen car here."

Hamish got to his feet. "I'm not here about stolen cars," he said. "I want to show you some photos and I want you to look at the folk in the photos and tell me if one of them called at your yard and asked for an old felt mat, like the kind you see under the bonnets of some engines, and two sparking plugs."

He looked at the man without hope. It was too

long a shot. "Funny that," said the owner slowly. "I call to mind someone asking me for thae things."

Hamish held out the photographs.

The man took them and led the way into the hut. He switched on the light and then with maddening slowness took a pair of glasses from his overall pocket and put them on his nose. He peered at the photographs.

"Aye," he said. "That's who ye want."

Hamish looked down. His finger was almost covering one face.

"My God!" said Hamish. "Are ye sure? Ye have to be awfy sure. If it's that one, man, I couldnae for the life o' me think why."

"Of course I'm sure," he said testily. "I can call tae mind every sod that comes in here. Came and asked fur sparking plugs and then fur the felt tae line the bonnet o' a car. A Renault it was."

Hamish took out a form he had brought with him and took down a statement and got the scrap yard owner to sign it. As he drove off, the sun was slipping below the horizon and the perpetual twilight of a northern summer lay across the countryside.

He drove a little way and pulled off the road and sat, thinking hard. Why?

And then, after an hour, all the little bits and pieces fell into place and he was looking at an almost complete picture. There was only one large piece missing and that was the reason for the death of Steel Ironside.

He called first at Dr. Brodie's, then at the minister's, back to the police station to make a few phone calls, and then made his way to the bungalow. P.C. Graham was still on duty. "You're going to cop it frae Donati," she jeered, "and I'm coming in tae watch."

Hamish ignored her and went on into the house. Mrs. Todd was busy at the kitchen sink. "They're all in the sitting room," she said.

Hamish walked into the sitting room. Crispin, Peter, and James were sitting together on the sofa. Alison was curled up in an armchair. Donati was sitting on a hard chair in the middle. MacNab and Anderson were over by the window.

Donati looked up briefly and his face hardened. "I'll deal with you later, Macbeth," he said. "Get outside and make sure no press get as far as the house."

"But—" began Hamish.

"I said, get outside!"

P.C. Graham sniggered and took up a position against the wall, anxious to stay and watch the interrogation. Hamish could stand guard on his own.

Hamish did not go outside. He went into the kitchen and pulled out a kitchen chair and sat down.

In his usual lazy, companionable way, he said, "Aye, it was a grand funeral. A fitting funeral for a lady like Mrs. Baird."

Mrs. Todd said nothing but continued to scrub pots with ferocious energy.

"She was a verra good woman as well," Hamish went on.

Mrs. Todd swung round. "Maggie Baird was a whore," she said viciously.

Hamish gave a little sigh and said quietly, "And you are the instrument of God."

She wiped her hands on her apron and slowly came and sat down opposite him. Hamish clasped his hands behind his head and looked dreamily at the ceiling. "It was those photographs of you in the army. You were in the army during the war and would know a lot about car engines. You were a chauffeur to a Colonel Wilson in the Royal Artillery, or so the village gossip goes. You burned that book of Maggie's. You read it and you burned it. I gather from Alison it was pretty hot stuff. Enough to turn that daft mind o' yours.

"Your husband took to the drink and you joined the Temperance Society and you neffer gave the man a day's peace till he drank himself to death. You asked Brodie to put 'heart attack' on the death certificate because you thought alcohol poisoning was a disgrace. He refused, but it was what else Brodie told you that shocked you. He told you your husband had venereal disease. Brodie told me that Mr. Todd had confessed to going with prostitutes from time to time in Aberdeen because he had had nothing in that line from you since your wedding night. Then I remembered the case of Mary MacTavish. She had an illegitimate child and Mr. Wellington said you made that lassie's life such hell she had to leave the village. When the minister reproached you for your lack of charity, you said you were doing God's work.

"Now, we come to Alison Kerr.

"She was a girl after your own heart, quiet and shy. But I gather you can hear everything in this house and so you listened at her bedroom door and that way you found out she was in bed with Peter Jenkins. You had committed murder once. And to my mind it was murder. You knew Maggie Baird had a weak heart. So you tampered with the brakes of Alison's car. She had become unclean and had to go. But when you managed to poison her mind against Peter Jenkins...oh, I'm sure that rubbish Alison was talking about that a man would never respect you after you had slept with him came from you...I think you decided to give her a reprieve. Then the pop singer. You didn't use the car but you could easily have cycled out or walked."

"You can't prove a thing," said Mrs. Todd.

"Oh, but I can," said Hamish, straightening up, his eyes hard and implacable and cold. "You went to the scrap yard at Brora and got the sparking plugs and the bit o' felt and the man there identified you from your photograph."

Mrs. Todd rose and went back to the sink and started scrubbing pots again.

"I'll tell you something else," said Hamish. "You're like Maggie Baird."

Mrs. Todd stopped scrubbing. "Never!" she said passionately.

"Yes, in a way. You see, when Maggie was all fat and tweedy and playing the country lady, I had an odd feeling that there was a pretty, flirtatious woman locked up inside all that fat, ready to come out like a butterfly coming out of a chrysalis. Inside that motherly outside of yours, Mrs. Todd, I see another woman: a thin, sharp, bitter, murderous woman."

"Havers," said Mrs. Todd calmly and opened a kitchen drawer.

Detective Jimmy Anderson was to say long afterwards that the biggest shock he ever had in his career was when Hamish Macbeth erupted from that kitchen and dived over the sofa and the three men sitting on it, pursued by Mrs. Todd who was waving a glittering bread knife. Galvanized into action, MacNab and Anderson and Donati grabbed hold of her while P.C. Graham twisted the bread knife out of her hand. She struggled and cursed, trying to escape, her eyes bulging with hate as she surveyed the lanky length of Hamish Macbeth rising from behind the sofa.

As they put the handcuffs on her, Hamish charged her with the attempted murder of Mrs. Margaret Baird. Then he said, "Why Steel Ironside? Why the pop singer?"

"Dirty man!" Mrs. Todd spat out the words. "He wore his shirts open the whole time showing all that nasty, nasty hair. Yes, I burned that book of hers. I knew men were filth but I never realised how filthy till I read it. Wallowing in filth. Filth!" she screamed, and she was still screaming while they led her outside.

"She's mad," whispered Alison.

"Yes," said Hamish wearily. "Barking mad and I never even noticed."

"Yaas," said James in his fake upper-class voice. "Of course, one never really looks at servants. I say, Alison, what about drinks all round? Thank God it's all over."

"Yes," said Alison, a little colour beginning to come into her pale face. "Yes, it's over and I'm safe." She flung her arms around Hamish. "Oh, thank you!"

Hamish looked across her head to Peter Jenkins and signalled with his eyes and Peter came up. Hamish pushed Alison gently into Peter's arms. "I'd best be off," he said.

He had parked his Land Rover on the road outside. The press had disappeared for the moment but he knew they would soon be back. P.C. Graham was standing morosely on duty.

"I suppose you think you're damned clever," she sneered.

Hamish looked at her, at the thin mouth and at the dislike in her eyes.

"You look beautiful when you're angry," he said. He jerked her into his arms and kissed her on the mouth. Then he walked off whistling.

Her voice followed him. "Why, Hamish! I never knew...I never guessed. Hamish, darling..."

Hamish threw one horrified look behind him and then ran to his Land Rover and drove off, breaking the speed limit all the way to Lochdubh.

At the police station, he fed Towser, locked up the hens for what was left of the night, and started to make himself some supper. And then the bell at the police station door sounded.

He walked up to it and shouted, "No comment" through the letter box.

"It's me, Donati," said a voice.

Hamish opened the door.

Donati walked past him and into the police office. "I'll need your notes, Macbeth. Was it a lucky guess?"

"No, I hae proof." Hamish fished in his pocket and brought out the statement by the owner of the scrap yard along with the photographs. Then he outlined what he had found out about Mrs. Todd's background.

"I should say 'good work,'" said Donati crisply, "but we could have found all this out much sooner if you had confided in me."

"But I only got the proof this evening," said Hamish.

"So you say. Well, type up your notes and let me have them along with this statement and the photographs. I shall be at the hotel until lunchtime tomorrow."

"Very well," said Hamish.

"Very well, what?"

"Very well, *sir*," said Hamish, resisting a longing to tell Donati exactly what he thought of him. But Donati might make things hot for him at headquarters in Strathbane and they might close down the police station again.

After Donati had left, he typed up his notes and put everything in an envelope.

The next morning, Donati simply took the envelope without a word of thanks. "We are now leaving for Strathbane," said Donati. "They will be raising that mini today. The divers will be along, but Anderson here will be in charge of that so there is nothing to take you away from your village duties."

Jimmy Anderson gave Hamish a sympathetic wink.

Hamish left the hotel and walked along the waterfront. The day was sunny and mild. Terror and murder had left the village. Mrs. Todd had been among them all for so long and yet none of them had realised she was unbalanced. But there were so many oddities in any village and no one ever stopped to wonder overmuch about them. There were at least four religious maniacs in Lochdubh apart from Mrs. Todd, and that was a small number for the Highlands where old-fashioned Calvinists still abounded and nothing moved on a Sunday for fear of incurring the wrath of God.

He took a deck chair out into the garden, stretched out in the sun, and fell asleep.

P.C. Macbeth had returned to his normal village duties.

Chapter Nine

Poverty is an anomaly to rich people. It is very difficult to make out why people who want dinner do not ring the bell.

—Walter Bagehot

As the shadows of violent murder withdrew from the village of Lochdubh, the weather took a turn for the better and long, lazy, hot days sent mist curling up from the sea loch and the mountains stood out stark and awesome against the bluest of skies. Purple heather blazed in all its glory on the hillsides and moorland and children collected wild raspberries from the hedgerows. The whole world seemed to have slowed almost to a halt as the sleepy village sank into a sunlit torpor.

Hamish was happy. Two whole weeks had passed since the murder and already it was fading from his mind. He had heard that Crispin and James had left the bungalow but that Peter Jenkins had stayed on, which explained, thought Hamish, why he had not been pestered by Alison. He had caught a fleeting glimpse of her when Peter had driven her through the village. He would have expected Alison to have bought another car, but perhaps the obsession for motoring had left her.

And then into this idyllic peace and quiet came Detective Chief Inspector Blair. Hamish was weeding the garden when the bulky shadow of Blair fell across him.

He straightened up, waiting for the inevitable remarks about lazy coppers but Blair surprised him by saying mildly, "Care tae come along tae the hotel for a drink, Hamish?"

"Sure," said Hamish, surprised. "I'll be with you in a tick. Just got to wash my hands."

He went indoors and quickly washed and scrambled into his uniform. Blair must be on a case. He could hardly have come all the way from Strathbane to pass the time of day.

They walked along together to the hotel, but Blair seemed to be reluctant to get to the point of his visit. He asked questions about the fishing and was it any good and then barely seemed to hear Hamish's replies. Once they were seated in a corner of the hotel bar, Hamish said, "Well, what's the case?"

"What? Oh, ah, I amnae on a case, Hamish. Fine day. Jist popped over to hae a wee chat."

"About what?" asked Hamish suspiciously.

"That nasty bugger, Donati."

"Oh, him," said Hamish. "What about him?"

"Well, I had it frae Anderson and MacNab that it was you that solved the murder case."

"You would get that from Donati's report," said Hamish sharply.

"Not a bit o' it."

"I saw the newspapers crediting him with solving the murder," said Hamish, "but I didn't think a man like Donati would take all the credit back at headquarters."

Blair gave him a long, bleak look.

Hamish shifted uncomfortably. "Now I come to think of it, that's what he *would* do."

"Aye, I got a look at his report. He said he had sent an officer, no name mentioned, to a scrap yard in Brora with photographs o' the suspects and thereby had obtained proof o' the Todd woman's guilt. When Anderson and MacNab finally told me, I felt it my duty to go to the super."

Hamish grinned. "It must hae choked ye to give me any praise."

"I'm a fair man," said Blair huffily. "But the super said that Donati's success had given him the transfer to Glasgow C.I.D. that he'd been angling after and it would rock the boat to start accusations flying around at this late date. So that scunner, Donati, went off south yesterday. Made my life a misery while he was in Strathbane. When they made him detective chief inspector, too, I knew it would only be a matter o' time before they demoted me."

"Then it's all to the good," said Hamish. "It's one way of getting rid of him. Thanks for telling me, anyway."

"I put the super's back up, ye see, because o' that Graham woman. The bitch. I really thought you'd gone off your trolley, Hamish, and assaulted her."

His voice was wheedling and conciliatory. Hamish looked at him sharply. Blair had been plotting his downfall for years. What was behind it all?

"So I hae been thinking...another drink, Hamish?"

"Yes, thank you. Whisky again, please."

Blair came back, carrying two doubles. Hamish blinked at this unusual generosity.

"So you didn't come all this way to tell me what you could hae told me on the phone," said Hamish. "What do you want?"

"It's like this." Blair hitched his chair closer to Hamish. "Ye seem tae attract murder. Now, say you get another big crime up here, I would be obliged if you could ask Strathbane for me."

"Oh." Hamish leaned back and studied Blair thoughtfully. "Why should I do that? At least Donati let me in on most of the case. You always send me off wi' a flea in my ear."

"Stands tae reason," blustered Blair. "You're only the village copper. Look! I promise to let ye in on the ground floor next time. Hae another drink."

"I haven't started this one yet. So what's behind it all?" Hamish looked at the big detective thoughtfully. Then he gave a slow smile. "Donati's gone. But there's another bright spark climbing up the ranks. Who is it?"

"This wee bastard, Finnock. Slimy wee bugger wi' a face like an arse," said Blair viciously. "It's yes, Mr. Daviot, and certainly, sir, and here are some flowers frae my garden fur your wife, sir, and lick your bum, sir. Yuch!"

"And I thought you were the best crawler in the business," said Hamish. Blair looked about to explode so he said placatingly, "Okay. I'll ask for you next time. But believe me, there cannae be a next time or we'll be changing the name o' the place from Lochdubh to Murder Village!"

AFTER BLAIR HAD finally driven off, Hamish returned to the police station. He was not used to drinking so much whisky in the middle of the day and he felt quite lightheaded.

He saw Alison and Peter Jenkins waiting outside the police station and turned to flee but it was too late. Alison had seen him.

As he approached the couple, he found he was staring at Alison in surprise. Her hair was shining and groomed in a new feathery cut. Gone were the thick glasses. She was expertly made up and she was wearing a blue cotton blouse and a pair of hot pants which revealed that she had very good legs indeed.

"Hey, Hamish!" said Alison cheerfully. "We've come to say goodbye."

"Come inside and I'll make some tea," said Hamish. "Where are you going?"

"I'm putting that bungalow up for sale. Peter and I are getting married." She held out a slim hand to show a diamond engagement ring.

"Congratulations!" said Hamish. Peter smiled modestly as if he had done something very clever.

"Where are you going to live?" asked Hamish, putting on the kettle.

"In London," said Alison. "Maggie owned a flat in Mayfair, in Charles Street. We're moving there. Peter wants to build up his advertising agency but I said to him, why bother? I mean, I've enough for both of us."

"It'll certainly be pleasant to be a gentleman of leisure," drawled Peter.

As Alison talked, Hamish watched her animated face. She and Peter would travel. There were so many countries she wanted to see.

Another butterfly, thought Hamish. It takes a weak man to make a strong woman. Alison was the one who was making all the decisions. Now that she was no longer interested in him, Hamish found her likeable.

"You haven't said anything about a new car," he said. "There certainly wasn't much of your mini left by the time they got it out to find the brakes had been tampered with."

"I don't want to drive anymore," said Alison with a shudder. "Peter can do all the driving from now on."

When they left, Hamish hoped Alison would manage to keep her fortune. A million pounds was no longer what it used to be and could be dissipated in an amazingly short space of time.

He was just settling down to enjoy some peace and quiet when he sensed an unease outside. He couldn't quite place it, but it was as if something bad had happened to alarm the village. He went round to his front garden and leaned on the fence.

Agnes, one of the maids from Tommel Castle,

was coming along the main street. She stopped to talk to the Currie sisters and Hamish heard the sisters' sharp exclamations of surprise and dismay.

Not another murder, he thought.

Agnes came nearer and he went to meet her. "What's happened?" he asked.

"It's himself. The colonel," gasped Agnes. "Called us all together last night and said he'd have to fire us all. He's lost all his money! What do you think happened?"

But Hamish was off and running for the Land Rover.

The castle door was open and Hamish walked in. Priscilla was crossing the hall. She stopped short at the sight of him and then she began to cry in a helpless way.

He put his arms around her and held her close, stroking her hair. When she had calmed down, he led her into the drawing room and sat down on the sofa with her, a comforting arm around her shoulders.

"What exactly happened?" he asked. "Agnes says he fired all the staff last night."

"Yes. He ... he ... called Mummy and me into the study and told us what was worrying him. As he talked, he got into one of his rages and I was afraid he might have a stroke. I feel so guilty." She dried her eyes firmly and gave a pathetic hiccup.

Mrs. Halburton-Smythe came into the room and stopped short at the sight of Hamish. Then she came forward and sat down, looking helplessly at him. "What are we to do, Hamish?" she said. There were two spots of colour on her pale cheeks and, unlike her daughter, she looked angry. "How could he do this to us?"

"Do what?" asked Hamish sharply.

Priscilla twisted her wet handkerchief in her hands. "That's why I feel so guilty," she said. "If it hadn't been for me this would never have happened. Do you remember John Harrington?"

"Your boyfriend who got done for insider trading? Yes."

"It turns out he had persuaded Daddy to let him have a vast sum to invest. Well, he didn't invest it. He skipped bail and the country with it."

"We've got nothing at all," said Mrs. Halburton-Smythe. "Nothing."

"Oh, dear." Hamish looked about him. "But you have the castle, and the estates alone must be worth a fortune."

"Yes, but everything costs a fortune to run," said Priscilla. "We can sell it. We have to sell it. But we're letting down the locals. Most of the staff apart from Jenkins, the butler, come in daily from the village but they rely on us for work. Daddy decided to fire the lot of them, not to mention the gamekeepers and gardeners and water bailiffs. We tried to tell him that somehow the place would need to be kept going until we could find a buyer, but he wouldn't listen."

Hamish thought quickly. "You might not have to sell it," he said.

Priscilla's mother looked at him in anguish. "Don't be stupid," she wailed. "Haven't we just told you we can't afford to run it?"

"There's a way you could," said Hamish, "and keep the staff. Where is the colonel?"

"In his study," said Priscilla. "But don't bother him, Hamish. The last person he will want to see is you."

"Be back in a minute," said Hamish with a grin. "I think he'll listen to me."

Mrs. Halburton-Smythe made a halfhearted attempt to stop him and then sank helplessly back in her chair.

Hamish went across the hall to the study and went in without knocking. Colonel Halburton-Smythe looked up and a purplish colour rose in his cheeks.

"Get out of here!" he roared. "Can't you see I've got enough to worry me without listening to the ditherings and bletherings of the village idiot?"

For one blissful minute, Hamish imagined how lovely it would be to tell the old horror to go to hell and fry. But then he thought of Priscilla. He pulled out a chair and sat down and smiled amiably at the colonel.

"I hae thought o' a grand way in which you could keep this house and the estates and the staff."

The colonel looked at him in silence, his eyes popping. Then he shrugged. "You're mad," he said.

"No, just listen. You've got grand fishing and shooting here," said Hamish. "Run it as a hotel. Wi' the shooting and the fishing, you could charge top rates. You've got a lot of bedrooms and most of them have their own bathroom."

The colonel stared at Hamish in silence, his small mouth hanging slightly open.

There was a soft knock at the door which then opened and Priscilla and her mother came into the study, both fearful in case Hamish's visit was driving the colonel into an apoplexy.

"Are you all right, dear?" asked the colonel's wife timidly. The colonel waved a peremptory hand for silence and sat staring off into the distance.

"What did you say?" whispered Priscilla fiercely in Hamish's ear. "He looks worse. He looks as if he has had a terrible shock."

The colonel suddenly brought both of his small

plump hands down on the desk with a thump that made them all jump.

"I've found a way to save Tommel Castle," he said.

"How? How can we?" gasped Mrs. Halburton-Smythe.

"We'll open it up as a hotel," said the colonel triumphantly. "Think of it. With the best shooting and the best fishing here, we'll make a fortune. We can invite our friends—"

"No," said Hamish quickly. "No friends. Mark my words, they'll look offended when you hand them the bill."

"Don't interrupt," snapped the colonel. "I have to make plans. Priscilla, get that secretary of mine here and get that architect chappie over from Strathbane."

"Do you think it will work?" asked Priscilla cautiously. "I mean, have we enough to keep going until we open for business?"

"Of course it will work," said her father robustly. "We've just enough to manage on until then. Trust me to come up with something. My chaps in the regiment always relied on me. Always a good man for thinking up ways out of a scrape. That was me."

Priscilla glanced at Hamish, who gave her a limpid look.

"Well, dear," said Mrs. Halburton-Smythe, "I am sure we are all grateful to Hamish for—"

"Stop wittering, woman, and tell the staff they can stay. Priscilla, get that architect on the phone. And you, Macbeth, have you nothing better to do?"

"I'm off," said Hamish cheerfully. "Grand to see you're your old horrible self."

Priscilla followed him out. "Honestly," she said furiously. "Daddy is the uttermost limit. That was your idea, Hamish."

"So long as you're all happy," said Hamish amiably. "I chust hope I haff not messed up your own career. I mean, surely they won't expect you to work in the hotel."

"They won't. But I'm going to," said Priscilla. "Can you imagine Daddy as mine host, Hamish? He'll forget they're paying guests and start insulting them!"

"I wass going to point out to him that he could have sold off his estates and kept the castle," said Hamish.

"It wouldn't have done any good. He wants to keep everything and you've found him a way to do it."

"Aye, that's what I thought. So long as he remembers that a hotel keeper can't go on like the lord of the manor."

"I doubt if he'll remember it for a moment," said Priscilla. "I'll probably have to run it myself and let him think he's doing it all on his own."

"You really don't mind?"

"Not really, Hamish. I was getting tired of London anyway."

"And I hope you don't feel guilty anymore," said Hamish. "Anyone daft enough to trust a rat like Harrington would be bound to lose their money to some fool sooner or later...or their heart."

Priscilla's cheeks turned pink. "That's below the belt, Hamish."

"Perhaps."

"Is Alison staying on in Lochdubh?" asked Priscilla, deliberately changing the subject.

"No, she's getting married to Peter and they're going to live in London. Let's hope that's the last of crime in Lochdubh." He told her about his visit from Blair.

"I don't think you're cut out to be a policeman," said Priscilla. "You let these detectives walk all over you. And for what? So that you can stay on as village constable and do as little as possible."

"That's right," said Hamish amiably.

"You are infuriating. Why don't you come in on this hotel lark?" She walked out of the hall with him and across the drive to the police Land Rover.

Hamish raised his hands in mock horror. "Tae my mind, working for your dad would be worse than working for Blair any day. What's the matter, Priscilla? Don't you like me the way I am?"

She looked down thoughtfully at her sandalled feet and did not reply.

"Well, cheerio," said Hamish. "See you around."

"Hamish, I..."

"Yes?" He turned around.

"Nothing," mumbled Priscilla.

As Hamish drove down to the police station, he found he was feeling very happy indeed, almost elated. It could surely not be because a moneyless, hotel-owning, working Priscilla was within his reach.

No, he told himself, that nonsense was over, but happiness bubbled inside him. He felt sure the days of crime were over for Lochdubh, and Priscilla would be just up the road all year round.

In the evening, he realised he had forgotten to buy anything for his dinner. He had sent, as usual, a good part of his monthly wage back to his mother and father and brothers and sisters over in Cromarty and so he could not afford to dine at the hotel. He ransacked his cupboards and came up with a solitary tin of baked beans.

"Beans it'll have tae be," he said to Towser. "And

no butcher's meat for you tonight, my boy. Dog food's all we've got." Towser hung his head and glared at the linoleum.

The phone rang. Hamish put down the cans and went to answer it. The caller was Priscilla.

"Hamish," she said. "There are a few points about this hotel business we would like to discuss with you. Could you possibly come to dinner this evening? Just the family and don't dress. You can even bring Towser."

Hamish accepted the invitation. He put down the phone and grinned at the receiver. "The auld man must hae been at the whisky," he said to Towser who had followed him. "Dinner at the castle for us. Come along."

He put on a clean shirt and tie and a pair of new trousers. He gave Towser a quick brush and then led the dog out to the police Land Rover.

"Times are changing, Towser," said Hamish Macbeth as he drove through the heathery twilight.

A watched pot never boils.

—Mid-nineteenth-century proverb

The fact that all the police forces in Scotland were to be amalgamated into one large force struck terror into police headquarters in Strathbane. It was said that all over Scotland three thousand auxiliary jobs would be lost, which would mean more work for the actual police themselves. Then they would start chopping heads of the very police force itself.

Only one man was happy about the news—Detective Chief Inspector Blair. Surely this might be the opportunity to get rid of Police Sergeant Hamish Macbeth and winkle him out of his cosy station in Lochdubh. He could not understand how Hamish had been able to hang on with local police stations closing down all over Scotland.

But he experienced a setback when he broached

the idea to his chief, Superintendent Daviot. "Suther- land is a huge county," said Daviot, "and it is surely economical to have Macbeth cover all of it."

"But most of the time, he and his sidekick, Fra- ser, just mooch around doing nothing," complained Blair.

"We have no proof of that," said Daviot severely. "You should be worried about your own job."

"Whit!"

"I am sure we will have officials soon crawling all over us to see what they can cut," said Daviot.

Blair took himself off to the pub to crouch over a double whisky and try to work out a plan. If he could prove that Hamish Macbeth did little, then he could send a report in to the new authorities. But who would be low enough to spy on Macbeth?

After another double whisky, his brain seemed to clear. Cyril Sessions was a fairly new consta- ble, nicknamed Romeo because of his good looks. Shortly after his arrival from Perth, Blair had uncovered evidence that Cyril had been enjoying the favours of a prostitute, without paying her a penny. She had finally cracked and reported Cyril. Blair got the complaint and confronted Cyril. Cyril had pleaded and begged and said he would do any- thing if Blair made the complaint go away.

Cunningly, Blair decided to keep this ally in the

bank, so to speak, until such time as he would need to draw on him. He phoned headquarters and asked Cyril to join him.

Women in the pub stared appreciatively at Cyril when he entered. He was of medium height with glossy black hair, blue eyes in a square handsome face, and a muscular figure.

"Sit down, my lad," said Blair. "I've a wee job for you. I want evidence that Hamish Macbeth in Lochdubh does bugger all when it comes to policing."

"Isn't that the man who's got a grand reputation for solving murders?"

"It was me that solved them," said Blair, "while that slimy toad took the credit. You owe me a favour, or do I need to remind you that I had to threaten that brass nail to keep her painted mouth shut?"

"Brass nail?"

"Where have you been? Brass nail. Screw. Get it? That prossy you were banging."

"Oh, aye. That."

"Aye, that. Here's what you've got tae do. Take a fishing holiday in Lochdubh and get photos of Macbeth lounging around. His policeman, Dick Fraser, often sleeps in a deck chair in the front garden. Get a good shot o' that. Macbeth doesn't know you, so you can get real close. Chat with the locals. Pick up gossip."

"I don't fish."

"Well, rambling or something like that. The highlands are fu' o' hairy-legged bastards farting ower the hills."

"When do I start?"

"Next week'll do. I want this done and dusted before numpties from the new police arrangement descend on us."

Cyril looked at him shrewdly. "Have you tried this before?"

Blair shifted his fat haunches on the barstool. He had, in fact, and it had ended with his spy nearly getting killed. But he had no intention of telling Cyril anything about it.

"No, just thought o' it," he said. "Get moving and fix that holiday."

HAMISH WAS ACTUALLY working at that moment. Lairg sheep sales are the biggest in Europe and he was policing them with Dick at his side. Because of the size of the sales, Strathbane had sent up two policemen to assist him. The importance of the yearly event meant that crofters were often dressed in the sort of finery people thought were the reserve of tourists: deer stalkers, tall crooks, kilts and sporrans.

Hamish and Dick strolled into the beer tent late

in the day and found their other two colleagues. "Everyone upset about the new Scottish police force?" asked Hamish, joining them.

"You can say that again," said one of them. "Take off the civilian staff, and think o' the extra paperwork."

"And how's my dear friend Blair?" asked Hamish.

The other policeman sniggered, "I think he's in lurv."

"Who's the lucky lady?"

"It's a bloke. Fairly new copper called Cyril Sessions. Real handsome chap. Blair's been seen drinking with him all over the place. Can't get enough of his company."

As THEY WALKED out of the beer tent, Dick said sententiously, "It does happen, you know."

"What does?" asked Hamish.

"Fellows when they get on a bit. They wake up to the fact that they prefer other blokes to their missus."

"Oh, aye? Well, the only love affair Blair's ever had is with the booze. He's plotting something."

"Do you mind if I hurry off?" said Dick anxiously. "I'm due down in Strathbane."

"Another quiz?"

"Aye, and the prize is a brand new Volvo."

"Off you go. Things are quiet here."

HAMISH SWITCHED ON the television that evening. Dick had such a reputation for winning quiz competitions that he was surprised they let him on.

The questions seemed to be very difficult. Six contestants were quickly whittled down to two, Dick and a shabby old man. And then Dick lost at the last question: how long does it take light from the moon to reach the earth?

The old man said quickly, "One-point-twenty-six seconds." There was a roll of drums and cheers from the audience as he was led to the gleaming new car.

Hamish waited up until a weary Dick arrived home. "Not like you to lose," said Hamish. "That must be the first time."

"I couldnae do it to him," said Dick.

"What?"

"He was an auld crofter. He'd never been on one of thae quiz shows before. The stories o' hardship he told me in the green room. It would ha' been wicked not to let the poor auld soul win."

"What was his name again?"

"Henry McQueen. Got a bittie o' a place outside Bonar Bridge."

"I wonder if there's anything on the computer about him," said Hamish.

"Why?"

"Just a hunch. I've got a feeling I saw him at the sheep sales."

Dick followed Hamish into the police office. Hamish switched on the computer and searched for Henry McQueen's name. "There's something here from last year's *Highland Times*," said Hamish, clicking it open. "There you are. I thought I'd heard of him. He took top price for his lambs two years running. You were conned. Oh, here's another link. Five years ago he came out top on *Mastermind*. Subject, the Epistles of St. Paul."

"I'll murder the auld creep," raged Dick.

"Oh, leave it. I'm sure he'll crop up again," said Hamish soothingly, "and then you can wipe the floor with him."

THE FOLLOWING DAY, Cyril checked into Mrs. Mackenzie's bed and breakfast on the waterfront at Lochdubh. He dumped his haversack in a small room and wondered how long he could put up with pretending to be a rambler, particularly as he had arrived in his car. He had pointed out to Blair that he was surely not going to be able to follow Macbeth around on foot.

The room was at the back of the house. It was cold. There was a meter on the wall with a sign saying that pound coins had to be deposited for electricity. The bed was narrow and covered in rough blankets under a pink candlewick spread. A print of Jesus feeding the multitude with loaves and fishes hung over the blocked-up fireplace. Underneath was the legend "His Eye Is on the Sparrow." On a rickety table by the bed was a large Bible. The room was fairly dark. Cyril popped a coin in the meter and switched on the light in a glass bowl above his head full of dead flies. He hung his clothes in the curtained alcove that served as a wardrobe. There was neither a phone nor a television set. The only reason, he thought, that she got any customers was because Mrs. Mackenzie charged cheap rates.

He decided to go out for a walk around the village and start work.

The day outside was warmer than his room. A pale October sun shone down on a row of white-washed cottages fronting the sea loch. It looked like a picture postcard. Cyril walked towards the harbour. He brightened when he saw a pub. He would start with a drink and see what he could find out from the locals. There was a silence when he entered. He ordered a vodka and tonic.

A small man in tight clothes materialised at his elbow and said, "Are you on holiday?"

"Yes," said Cyril. "I'm Jamie Mackay up from Perth."

"Archie Maclean," said the little man.

"Let me buy you a drink," said Cyril, "and maybe we could sit over at that table by the window. I'd like to get to know a bit about the village."

Archie ordered a double whisky. Cyril realised that Blair had said nothing about paying for his work. Conversation rose again as they made their way to the table.

"So what are you doing here?" asked Archie.

"I came up by car, but I might do a bit of walking."

Archie's sharp blue eyes in his nut-brown face dropped to look at Cyril's highly polished black shoes. "I hope you've got boots with you," he said. "You won't get far in those."

"Yes, I've got boots," said Cyril. He wondered why the little man wore such tight clothes, not knowing that Archie's wife washed all his clothes so that they shrank.

"So, much crime around here?" asked Cyril.

"No, it's fair quiet."

"I saw a police station. Not much for a copper to do up here."

"Hamish Macbeth, the police sergeant, covers a big part o' Sutherland," said Archie. "He's got a lot tae do. Thanks for the drink, laddie. Got tae go."

*   *   *

HAMISH WAS SEATED at the kitchen table when Archie burst through the door. "What's up?" asked Hamish.

"'Member the time when that scunner Blair put a copper on yer tail to report on ye?"

"As if it were yesterday," said Hamish. "Has he sent another?"

"Could be," said Archie, sitting down at the table. "Could I hae wan o' your espresso coffees? The wifie doesnae hold wi' coffee."

"That's Dick's machine. I don't know how to operate it. I'll fetch him. He's sleeping in the garden."

Hamish strolled round to the front of the police station just in time to see the tall figure of Cyril snapping a photograph of Dick asleep in his deck chair. He nipped round onto the road and confronted Cyril. "What's so special about a photograph of a man in a deck chair?" asked Hamish.

"I'm a bit of an amateur photographer," said Cyril. "I thought I'd enter it for a competition and call it 'Sleeping Policeman.'"

"Visiting?"

"Yes. Good place for walks."

"Where are you staying?" asked Hamish.

"Mrs. Mackenzie's. I'll be getting along."

Cyril strode off. Hamish stared after him. Then he went into the office and phoned detective Jimmy Anderson.

"How are things up in peasantville?" asked Jimmy.

"Weird."

"It's aye weird up there."

"There's this fellow turned up and took a photo of Dick asleep in the garden. Handsome chap with curly black hair, tall, blue eyes, little half-moon scar above the right eye, but with policeman's shoes on and black socks. Says he's going to be going for walks. Anyone missing from headquarters that looks like that?"

"There's one smarmy bastard who sucks up to Blair. Cyril Sessions."

"I knew it!" exclaimed Hamish. "Blair is out to get proof that there's no crime up here. I'll get that photo back somehow."

Hamish woke Dick up and explained the situation. He ended by saying, "Let's see if we can lose the cheil for an hour. Give Archie a mug o' espresso first."

They walked over to the harbour fifteen minutes later, where Archie Maclean was sitting on a bollard, rolling a cigarette. "No tourists today?" asked Hamish. Fishing stocks were dwindling, and so

Archie supplemented his income by taking tourists on trips round the loch.

"I've only got a couple. They'll be along in a minute."

"Do me a favour. Yon chap you met in the pub is one o' Blair's snoops. He'll be hanging around. He's staying at Mrs. Mackenzie's. Offer him a free trip in your boat."

"Aye, right. Want me to tip him ower the side?"

"No, just keep him away. If he's got his camera with him, try to stage an accident to the camera that makes it look as if it's his fault."

ARCHIE SCURRIED OFF. He found Cyril outside Mrs. Mackenzie's. Cyril was delighted to accept. It would be a chance to find out more about Macbeth.

Hamish stood at his living-room window, watching, until he saw the fishing boat sail out into the loch. Then he hurried along to Mrs. Mackenzie's bed and breakfast.

Before he got there, he met the Currie sisters, twins Nessie and Jessie, on the waterfront. They were very much alike. Although the day was sunny, there was a nip in the air, and so they had reverted to their winter wear of camel-hair coats, headscarves, and brogues.

"Grand day," said Hamish. "Have you seen the newcomer?"

"We have that," said Nessie. "Like a fillum star."

"Fillum star," echoed the Greek chorus that was Jessie.

"It's refreshing to find a young man who kens so much about the Bible," said Hamish. "He's out with Archie, but when he gets back, you should invite him to tea. Right religious, he is."

"We'll do that," said Nessie. "It will be nice to talk to a clean young man instead o' a lazy philanderer like yourself."

"Like yourself," came her sister's echo.

Hamish walked on and knocked at the door of the bed and breakfast. Mrs. Mackenzie was a small woman wearing a flower-patterned overall with her hair tied up in a headscarf. The lines on her face were permanently set in disapproval.

"Whit?" she demanded.

"I would like a look at the newcomer's room," said Hamish. "We've had a tip-off."

"Then he can pack his bags and get out."

"No, no," said Hamish soothingly. "Don't tell him I called. Chust a routine enquiry. You don't want to go losing a paying customer at this time of year. Chust a wee peek in his room."

"Oh, all right. Top o' the stairs on the left. The door isnae locked. I was up there cleaning."

Hamish nipped up the stairs and into Cyril's room.

There was a computer lying on the bed, but what he wanted was the camera. There was no sign of it. He could only hope that Archie would find a way to get rid of it.

ARCHIE LET HIS mate, Ally Harris, take the wheel while he pointed out various landmarks to the two tourists, a husband and wife, and Cyril. Cyril was standing at the side of the boat, his camera slung round his neck.

Moving behind him, Archie took out a sharp knife and sliced almost through the strap at the back of Cyril's neck.

He said, "If youse will look ower the side, that's where the kelpie is supposed tae live."

"What's a kelpie?" asked the female.

"It's a creature that appears as a sea horse and sometimes changes into a beautiful wumman," said Archie. "It goes after wee bairns. It gets them to stroke it and it's adhesive and when they stick to it, it drags them down into the loch and eats them. It's supposed to live right down there. Lean right ower and you'll maybe see it."

Cyril and the tourists leaned over. "There is something down there," said Cyril excitedly. A black shape could be seen moving in the murky depths. His camera was swinging from his neck by the strap. Just as he was reaching for it, the strap broke and his camera dropped down into the water.

A seal surfaced and stared up at them as Cyril let out a wail of dismay.

"You should ha' got yourself wan o' thae wee yins you can carry in your pocket," said Archie. "I hivnae seen wan like that in years. If you go to Patel's shop, you can buy wan o' thae cheap throw-away ones."

"It was a friend's camera," said Cyril. He cursed Blair, who had given him an old Rolleiflex camera out of storage at headquarters, saying it was better than any newfangled one. He did have a Canon pocket one inside his jacket. At least he would be more comfortable using that.

ARCHIE TELEPHONED HAMISH to say that Cyril's camera was now somewhere at the bottom of the loch, and Hamish heaved a sigh of relief.

Before, when he had been under threat, he had manufactured a crime wave with the help of the locals. But Hamish was feeling lazy, enjoying the rare good weather of the autumn.

CYRIL HAD READ up on Hamish's successful cases and knew that several had taken place in the town of Braikie. The following day, he decided to visit the town, hoping the residents there might have less favourable ideas about Hamish than the villagers had. He had gone to the village stores and after leaning on the counter, talking about the weather, he had asked the owner, Mr. Patel, what he thought of the local policeman. Mr. Patel had smiled and launched on a paean of praise about Hamish.

Cyril had then gone to the Italian restaurant for dinner and quizzed the waiter, Willie Lamont. His heart sank when it turned out that Hamish was godfather to Willie's child. Was no one going to criticise the man?

But in Braikie, his hopes sank lower. The people he talked to did not know Hamish personally but knew his reputation for solving murders and seemed to be proud to have such a policeman looking after them.

He was passing the library when he noticed a sign outside saying there were books for sale. Cyril decided to buy some light reading and walked into the Victorian gloom of the building.

Hetty Dunstable, the librarian, saw a handsome man looking around and teetered forward on her high heels. "Can I help you?"

Cyril saw a small, thin woman in her early forties wearing a nearly transparent white blouse over a tight skirt. She had a small, pinched face and bulging brown eyes. Cyril thought sourly that she looked like a rabbit with myxomatosis. But he gave his most charming smile and said, "I saw that you had books for sale."

"Yes, they're over here," said Hetty, leading the way to a wooden bench. "These are the ones that are too damaged to remain on the shelves. Are you new to the area?"

"Just on holiday," said Cyril. "I'm over in Lochdubh."

"Keep clear of the police station. Hamish Macbeth is useless."

"I'd like to hear more," said Cyril. "I enjoy a bit of gossip with a pretty girl. When do you get off?"

"We close up in ten minutes."

"Let's go for a drink."

"Yes, I would love that," said Hetty.

HETTY HAD NO intention of telling this gorgeous man her real reason for disliking Hamish. She had once invited Hamish to a party at her flat after having met him on one of his investigations. Hamish was not interested. But she had drunk too much and had thrown herself at him, calling him her darling. Hamish had gently pushed her away and gone home. Her friends teased her about it until she began to think Hamish had wronged her. She told them so many times that Hamish had led her on that she began to believe it.

CYRIL WAS OFTEN seen in Hetty's company in the following days. Then, to Hetty's dismay, he said he would be too busy to see her. Hetty began to feel guilty. She was sure Cyril was spying on Hamish and wondered if he was a villain. She had made up a lot of malicious stories about Hamish's laziness. If anything happened to Hamish, the investigation would lead back to her.

She at last phoned Hamish and said someone called Jamie Mackay had been asking a lot of questions about him.

"Don't worry," said Hamish. "I know all about him," correctly guessing that Jamie was Cyril.

"What will you do?" asked Hetty.

"Take my shotgun and blow the bugger's head off," said Hamish and rang off.

"LET'S GIVE CYRIL something to do tomorrow," Hamish said to Dick. "We'll race off tomorrow up north and give the lad something to chase. The beasties are getting fat. They need some exercise."

Hamish's "beasties" consisted of a wild cat called Sonsie and a dog called Towser. "I'll get a picnic ready," said Dick.

Hamish felt a stab of irritation. He wished Dick would not be so—well—*domesticated*. He felt Dick was taking the place of a possible wife, and Hamish often dreamed of marriage. His love affair with television presenter Elspeth Grant had recently fallen through. He had once been engaged to Priscilla Halburton-Smythe, daughter of the retired colonel who owned the Tommel Castle Hotel. But Priscilla's sexual coldness had caused him to break off the engagement.

AT THAT MOMENT, Cyril was ensconced in the Currie sisters' parlour, balancing a cup of tea on one knee. He had hoped the sisters would give him some gossip about Hamish, but they seemed hell-bent on quizzing him about the King James Version of the Bible.

"Beautiful words," said Nessie, " 'I am the voice of one crying in the wilderness.' "

"I couldn't agree more," said Cyril, ignoring Jessie's echo. He thought, If I don't get out of this damn place soon I'll go mad. "You were saying something about the local policeman."

"No, I wasn't," said Nessie.

"Bit of a layabout, is he?"

"We do not gossip in this village," said Nessie righteously. "Pass me the Bible, Jessie, and we'll hear this nice young man read to us."

It was a large Victorian Bible, illustrated with steel engravings. Feeling trapped, Cyril began to read, and, as he read, he began to experience a strange feeling of doom. His mobile phone suddenly rang, and he grabbed it out of his pocket. It was Blair, asking if there was any progress.

"Can't talk now, Mother," said Cyril. "I'll call you later." He rang off.

"You shouldn't cut your mother off like that," chided Nessie.

"How right you are." Cyril stood up and put the Bible and his cup on the table. "I'll get back to my digs and call her from there."

"We'll see you in the kirk on Sunday," said Nessie.

If I'm still alive and not dead with boredom, thought Cyril, making his escape.

"WHERE ARE WE off to?" asked Dick the next morning as he climbed into the Land Rover beside Hamish.

"Do you know Sandybeach?"

"No, where's that?"

"Tiny little place up north of Scourie. Grand place for a picnic. I'll put the siren on and get Cyril chasing us."

"It's only seven in the morning," said Dick. "Think he'll be up yet?"

"Probably not. But I've phoned Jimmy. Blair's bound to ask if there's been a report of a crime, so I told him to say there was a burglary at Sandybeach."

"So what do we do if the scunner catches up with us?"

"He won't. It's so quiet up there, you can hear a car coming for miles. We'll take off for somewhere else."

THE SOUND OF the siren woke Cyril. He tumbled out of bed and dashed to the window, opened it, and hung out. He could just see the Land Rover racing out over the humpbacked bridge. He scrabbled into his clothes and phoned Blair, asking him to find out where Hamish had gone.

He had gone a mile out of Lochdubh when Blair rang. "Burglary at a place called Sandybeach."

"Where's that?"

"How should I know? Look at a map."

Cyril programmed his sat-nav and set off in pursuit. He hurtled along the one-track roads, blind to the beauty all around him. Purple heather blazed on the flanks of the soaring mountains. Rowan trees shone with bloodred berries. Above, the sky was an arch of blue. At one point, he thought he heard the sound of another driver behind him and suddenly stopped, switched off his engine, rolled down the windows, and listened. But there was nothing to be heard but the mournful call of a curlew.

Cyril crouched over the wheel and drove on.

Sutherland, the southland of the Vikings, is the most underpopulated county in the British Isles. The west coast has the most dazzling scenery. But to Cyril, it was an odd foreign landscape, alien, far from the bustle and crowds of Strathbane.

At long last, he saw a signpost pointing the way to Sandybeach.

"The end of the road," said Cyril, not knowing that, for him, it was.

SAVOR THE FLAVORS OF SCOTLAND—
WITH ANOTHER
HAMISH MACBETH MYSTERY
BY **M. C. BEATON!**

*Please turn the page
for a preview of*

Death of Yesterday

Morag Merrilea was an art student, earning money in her summer holidays by working as a secretary for Shopmark Fashions in Cnothan in the Scottish county of Sutherland. She was English and considered herself a cut above her fellow workers. She was highly unpopular. Her appearance was unprepossessing. She had lank brown hair and rather prominent green eyes. But she had a passion for art and for studying faces.

Shopmark Fashions was a new factory on the outskirts of the village, risen out of an old derelict Victorian furniture store. Cnothan was a grim place, with one main street running down to a man-made loch over which towered the grey walls of a hydro-electric dam.

Morag had taken the job because she had dreamt of a romantic highland village, and had never quite got over the culture shock of being in Cnothan where the sour locals took pride in "keeping themselves to themselves."

SHE SAT IN her usual corner of the Highlander pub one Saturday evening with her sketchbook, busily drawing the faces of people in the pub, and, also, the face of someone looking in at the window. Morag always drank alone. The other employees of the factory drank at a pub down on the lochside and, strangely enough, Morag's solitary drinking was not remarked on because of her unpopularity and the locals shying away from any mention of her.

Although not particularly imaginative, she seemed that particular evening to feel the remoteness, the very foreignness of Sutherland pressing in on her, a claustrophobic sense that the great towering mountains were creeping closer across the heathery moors. The result was, she drank more than usual. The pub was quite full with forestry workers, crofters, and the unemployed. Morag was brilliant at drawing faces and felt the very act of drawing people and putting them on paper put them in her power.

At one point, she went to the lavatory. When she returned, she found her sketchbook was missing.

She complained to the barman and to everyone around. Getting nothing in reply but blank stares, she downed her drink and made for the door. Morag collapsed outside and was taken to hospital.

After she came awake the following morning and received a lecture from a young doctor on the evils of drink, Morag was gripped with a sudden fear that she might be an alcoholic. She had drunk four pints of beer and assumed she had experienced a blackout. She could not remember yesterday evening at all.

She did have one friend at Hornsey Art College, where she had studied. She phoned her friend, Celia Hedron, and told her about losing her memory.

Celia said sharply, "Have you considered that someone might have slipped you a date rape drug? That blacks you out so you can't remember things."

This dramatic solution appealed to Morag, who did not like to think she was a common alcoholic. She dithered for a week before catching a bus from Cnothan and presenting herself at the police station in Lochdubh. She had been told that the police sergeant, Hamish Macbeth, was also responsible for policing Cnothan—along with vast tracts of Sutherland.

HER FIRST IMPRESSION of Hamish Macbeth was a bad one. When she arrived, he was up on a ladder clearing out the guttering. His lazy constable, Dick

Fraser, a plump man with a grey moustache, was sleeping peacefully in the front garden on a deck chair.

"You!" shouted Morag. "Get down here immediately. I have a crime to report."

Hamish came slowly down the ladder. She saw a tall man with flaming red hair and hazel eyes.

"What seems to be the problem?" he asked.

Morag threw back her head and declared, "I have been drugged, raped, and my sketchbook has been stolen."

"Then you'd better come ben to the office," said Hamish mildly.

"Whassat?" mumbled Dick and went back to sleep.

Hamish led the way in at the side door, through the kitchen and into his small office, where he pulled out a chair for her. He wrote down the details of her addresses in Cnothan and London along with her phone numbers at home and work.

"It's like this," said Morag. She gave him her view of what had happened, along with details of her age, twenty-three, and her work as a secretary at the clothes factory.

"And when exactly did this take place?" asked Hamish.

"Last Saturday week."

Hamish had been taking notes. He put down his pen. "If you were drugged with some date rape drug, it would no longer be in your system. Were you checked for signs of rape?"

"Well, no."

"I think we should go to the hospital right away and have you checked."

Morag bit her lip. She had examined herself and knew there were no signs of bruising or forced entry. "I can't be bothered," she said.

"Then I don't see what you expect me to do," said Hamish patiently.

"You are a moron," said Morag. "You could at least make some push to get my sketchbook back—that is if you ever get off your arse and do anything."

"What were you sketching?"

"Faces of people in the pub. Oh, and someone who looked in at the window."

"Are you any good?" asked Hamish bluntly.

She opened her large handbag and pulled out a small sketchpad and handed it to him.

His interest quickened. She was very good indeed.

"I'll need to take a note of who was in the pub. Can you remember any names?"

"They're all just faces to me—Angus this and Jimmy that. I do not consort with the local peasantry.

The factory staff drink at the Loaning down on the loch."

"With an attitude like that," said Hamish, the sudden sibilance of his accent showing he was annoyed, "I'm fair astounded that someone didnae try to bump you off instead of chust slipping something in your drink."

"You're as useless as the rest of . . ."

"Calm down, lassie. I hae this idea . . ."

"Wonders will never cease."

"Oh, shut up and listen for once in your life. I know a hypnotist down in Strathbane. He might be able to put you under and restore some o' your memory."

Morag's protruding eyes gleamed. The drama of such a suggestion appealed to her, along with the idea of rattling the cage of whoever had drugged her drink.

"I'll make an appointment and let you know," said Hamish.

HAMISH WONDERED AS he set off for Strathbane later that day with Dick why he was even bothering to help such an unlovely character as Morag Merrilea. He cursed himself for not having asked exactly how much she had to drink. She could simply have had an alcoholic blackout.

Still, he reminded himself, he wasn't doing

anything else at the moment. The summer was unusually warm with those nasty biting midges of the Highlands out in force. Patel's, the local shop in Lochdubh, had sold out of insect repellent.

As they mounted a crest of the road, Dick said, "Every time I see Strathbane, I'm right glad I'm out of it."

Strathbane was a blot on the beauty of Sutherland. Once a busy fishing port, it had died when the fishing stocks ran out. Drugs arrived, and it became a town with an air of dirt and desolation.

"I don't like this idea of a hypnotist," said Dick. "Sounds awfy like black magic."

"Och, even Strathbane police use Mr. Jeffreys from time to time."

"Did they say they would pay his bill?"

Hamish shifted uncomfortably in the driver's seat. He knew that Detective Chief Inspector Blair, the bane of his life, would have put a stop to it.

"It's fine," he said airily. "He'll just send in his bill as usual."

DICK WAS DISAPPOINTED in Mr. Jeffreys. He had expected to meet an elderly guru.

But Jeffreys was only in his thirties, a thin man with brown hair in a ponytail, dressed in torn jeans and a T-shirt.

"Let me see," said Jeffreys. "I can fit her in at three o'clock next Saturday."

Hamish phoned Morag on her mobile. She was delighted. "Wait till those bastards in the pub hear about this!"

"I wouldnae go around shooting your mouth off," cautioned Hamish. "I'll collect you on Saturday and take you to Strathbane."

IN THE THREE days leading up to Saturday, Hamish and Dick pottered around the police station. To Dick Fraser, a portly man with a grey moustache, it was paradise. Viewed as useless by headquarters in Strathbane, he had been relocated to Lochdubh. He was a quiz addict, appearing on television quiz shows, and the kitchen in the police station gleamed with his winnings—an espresso coffee making machine, a dishwasher, a new washing machine, and a new microwave.

The single and widowed ladies of the village began to regard him as prime husband material, but Dick showed no interest, preferring to dream in a deck chair in the front garden by day and watch television in the evenings.

He was roused from his lethargy on Saturday by Hamish. "We'd better go and pick up yon Morag female," said Hamish. "Get your uniform on."

Morag rented a flat in a Victorian villa on the

edge of Cnothan. When Hamish rang her doorbell, there was no reply. Morag's flat was on the top floor. He stood back and looked up. The curtains were open but there was no sign of anyone moving about.

"Silly cow," he muttered. "I'm sure she wouldnae have forgotten." He rang the landlady's bell.

Mrs. Douglas, the landlady, opened the door. She was a small round woman with thick glasses and an untidy thatch of grey hair.

"Whit now?" she demanded.

"We've come to collect Miss Merrilea," said Hamish patiently. "Is herself at home?"

"Dinnae ken."

"Would you please go and look?"

Grumbling, she shuffled off up the stairs. They waited in the warm sunlight.

At last she reappeared and handed Hamish a postcard. "This was stuck on her door," she said.

Typed neatly on a postcard was: "Gone to London. Will be in touch." It was not signed.

"I don't like this," said Hamish. "Would you mind showing us her flat?"

"Have ye a warrant?"

"No, I haff not!" said Hamish. "But if you don't let me in and show me her flat, I'll come back here with a warrant and I will turn this whole damn place upside down, including your premises."

"Here, now, no need for that," she said, thinking of the cash undeclared to the taxman hidden under her mattress. "I'll get the key."

They followed her into a shadowy hall lit with coloured harlequin diamonds of light from the sun shining through the stained-glass panel on the front door.

Dick eyed the steep stairs. "I'll be waiting for ye outside, sir," he said to Hamish.

"Oh, all right," said Hamish crossly.

He followed Mrs. Douglas as she panted up the stairs. She inserted a key into a door on the top landing. "There's no need for you to wait," said Hamish. "I'll bring you down the key when I've finished."

The flat consisted of a small living room, a cell of a bedroom, a kitchen unit behind a curtain, and a shower. The living room contained a small card table laden with artist's materials and two hardback chairs by the window. There was a dingy print of The Stag at Bay over the empty fireplace. One battered armchair was beside the fireplace facing a small television set. Planks on bricks along one wall supplied bookshelves.

Hamish went in to the bedroom. He opened the wardrobe. A few skirts and blouses hung there and a winter coat. On top of the wardrobe was a large suitcase. He hauled it down and opened it up. It was empty. He put it back and then opened a chest of drawers. There were various surprisingly saucy items of lingerie: thongs and stockings with lace tops.

He sat down on the bed and looked round. She might have had a backpack of some kind to take a few clothes with her. There was no sign of a handbag, passport, or wallet.

He locked up and went downstairs to where Mrs. Douglas was waiting in the hall. "Did she have a car?" he asked, handing over the keys.

"No, she had a bike."

"And where does she keep it?"

"Just outside. But it's no' there."

"When did you last see her?"

"Cannae bring tae mind."

"Think!"

"Oh, I mind now. It was yesterday morning. Herself was just off tae work."

"Was she carrying a suitcase or any sort of luggage?"

"No. She just got on her bike and went off, same as ever."

Hamish felt uneasy. He put the postcard in a forensic bag and went out to join Dick.

"We'd better check where she works," he said. "I've got a bad feeling about this."

* * *

AT SHOPMARK FASHIONS, they found that Morag worked as secretary to the boss, Harry Gilchrist. Mr. Gilchrist kept them waiting ten minutes, which Hamish put down to the usual pompous Scottish boss's way of trying to seem important.

Mr. Gilchrist was a tall thin man in his forties. He had thick black hair in a widow's peak above a sallow face and wet brown eyes.

"Working on Saturday?" asked Hamish.

"Work never stops," said Gilchrist. "What do the police want with me?"

"Did Morag Merrilea turn up for work yesterday?"

"As a matter of fact, she didn't. I meant to send someone to check on her on Monday if she was still absent."

"She left a postcard on the door of her flat saying she had gone to London."

"Isn't that just typical of staff these days!" raged Gilchrist. "Well, if you come across her, tell her she's fired."

"Did she say anything about going to see a hypnotist?"

"No. A hypnotist? Why?"

Hamish explained about the suspected drugged drink and the missing sketchbook.

"Oh, that? She was complaining about that all over the place. She did drink a fair bit. She was in the habit of making things up."

"Is there anyone she was close to?"

"She kept herself to herself."

Like the whole of bloody Cnothan, thought Hamish.

DICK AND HAMISH next went to the Highlander pub. Pubs all over Britain had been smartened up with restaurants and pleasant décor, but the Highlander had been unmoved by time. There was one dim room with scarred tables and rickety chairs. The walls were still brown with nicotine from the days before the smoking ban. The only food on offer was in a glass case on the counter: tired-looking sandwiches and a solitary mutton pie.

Hamish recognised the barman and owner, Stolly Maguire. Stolly was polishing a glass with a dirty rag when they approached him. He was a thickset man with a bald head with a tank top strained over a beer belly.

Hamish explained they were trying to find out the whereabouts of Morag Merrilea.

"Thon artist?" said Solly. "Havenae seen her. Usually comes in Saturday evening."

"Two Saturdays ago," said Hamish patiently, "did

you notice anyone approaching her table when she went to the toilet?"

"Naw. It was fair busy."

Hamish turned round and surveyed the customers, a mixture of crofters, shepherds, builders, and the unemployed.

"Which one of them was here two Saturdays ago?"

"I cannae mind," said Stolly. "Ask them? I saw her collapsing outside the door and phoned for an ambulance."

So Hamish and Dick went from table to table to receive surly answers to the effect that they had seen her on that Saturday but hadn't noticed anyone taking her sketchbook or putting something in her drink.

But a youth with greasy hair said he had noticed a stranger. "Can you describe him?" asked Hamish. "What is your name?"

"Fergus McQueen."

"Well, Fergus, what did he look like?"

"Hard tae tell. He had wan o' thae baseball caps pulled right down. Small and skinny."

"What was he wearing?"

"Black T-shirt, black jeans."

"The cap. Did it have a logo on it?"

"Naw. It was dark green with an orange stripe."

"Give me your address. We may want you to come to Strathbane and help a police artist make a sketch."

BACK AT LOCHDUBH, Hamish sat down at the computer in the police station office and sent over a report. He felt uneasy. It was too much of a coincidence that she should disappear when she had an appointment with the hypnotist.

To his amazement, he got a call from Detective Sergeant Jimmy Anderson later that day. "Blair's decided to look into it," he said.

"Why? I thought he'd delight in shooting the whole thing down," said Hamish.

"I think he feels if there is a crime, then he wants to be the one to solve it. You've stolen his glory too many times."

"I'd better get back to Cnothan and join him."

"He says you're to sit tight and look after your sheep and leave it to the experts."

Hamish groaned. He knew that Blair's blustering, bullying tactics would make the locals clam up even more.

HAMISH WAITED GLOOMILY for the inevitable. Sure enough, it came later with an e-mail from Blair telling him it was a wild-goose chase and to stop wasting police time and, furthermore, never again try to employ the hypnotist without first getting clearance.

Undeterred, Hamish went back to Cnothan, knocking on doors, questioning one after the other without success.

He was furious when he returned to Lochdubh to receive a phone call from Superintendent Daviot. The locals in Cnothan had complained of police harassment. Blair had found nothing. Hamish was to leave it all alone.

THE WEATHER WAS unusually hot. Three weeks after the disappearance of Morag Merrilea, two men were loading bales of T-shirts onto a lorry outside Shopmark Fashions when they suddenly stopped their work.

"Thon's an awfy smell from that bale," said one, "and it's heavy, too."

"Better cut it open," said his companion. "There's maybe a dead animal inside."

They sliced the twine that held the bale and unrolled it.

The dead and decomposing body of Morag Merrilea rolled out and lay under the eye of the glaring sun.

SAVOR THE FLAVORS OF SCOTLAND—
WITH ANOTHER
HAMISH MACBETH MYSTERY
BY **M. C. BEATON!**

*Please turn the page
for a preview of*

Death of a Nag

*O the disgrace of it!—The scandal,
the incredible come-down!*

—Sir Max Beerbohm

Hamish Macbeth awoke to another day. His dog, Towser, was lying across his feet, snoring rhythmically. Sunlight slanted through the gap in the curtains. The telephone in the police office part of the house shrilled and then the answering machine clicked on. He should rise and go and find out what it was. It was his duty as a police constable of the village of Lochdubh and part of the surrounding area of the county of Sutherland. But all he wanted to do was pull the duvet over his head and go back to sleep.

He could not really think of any good reason for getting up to face the day.

He had, until his demotion from sergeant back to

constable and the end of his engagement with Priscilla Halburton-Smythe, daughter of a local hotelier, been very popular, a happy state of affairs he had taken for granted. But somehow the story had got about that he had cruelly jilted Priscilla, she who had been too good for him in the first place, and so, when he went about his duties, he was met with reproachful looks. Although Chief Superintendent Peter Daviot had also been angry with him over the end of the engagement, that was not why Hamish had been demoted. He had solved a murder mystery by producing what he firmly believed was the body of the murdered man to elicit a shock confession from the guilty party. The ruse had worked, but he had had the wrong body. It had turned out to be a fine example of Pictish man and the police were accused of being clod-hopping morons for having so roughly handled and used such a prime exhibit. Someone had to be punished, and naturally that someone was Hamish Macbeth.

Hamish was not an ambitious man. In fact, he was quite happy with his lot as ordinary police constable, but he felt the displeasure of the village people keenly. His days before his disgrace had pleasantly been given up to mooching around the village and gossiping. Now no one seemed to want to spend the time of the day with him, or that was the way it seemed to his gloomy mind. If Priscilla, whom Hamish considered remarkably unaffected by the end to the romance, had stayed around to demonstrate that fact, then he would not be in bad odour. But she had left to stay with friends in Gloucestershire for an extended visit, so as far as the villagers were concerned, Hamish had driven her off and she was down in "foreign" parts, nursing a broken heart.

Mrs. Halburton-Smythe did not help matters by shaking her head and murmuring "Poor Priscilla" whenever Hamish's name was mentioned, although what Mrs. Halburton-Smythe was sad about was that she was beginning to believe that her cool and aloof daughter did not want to marry anyone.

With a groan, Hamish made the effort and got up. Towser gave a grumbling sound in the back of his throat and slid to the floor and padded off towards the kitchen.

Hamish jerked back the curtains. The police station was on the waterfront and overlooked the sea loch, which lay that morning as calm as a sheet of glass.

He washed and dressed and went through to the police office. The message was from headquarters in Strathbane reminding him he had not sent in a full statement about a break-in at a small hotel on the road to Drum. He ambled into the kitchen and made himself a breakfast of bread and cheese, for he had forgotten to light the stove. Priscilla had presented him with a brand-new electric cooker, but he had childishly sent it back.

He fed Towser and stood on one leg, irresolute, looking like a heron brooding over a pond. Depression was new to him. He had to take action, to do something to lift it. He could start by typing that report. On the other hand, Towser needed a walk.

The phone began to ring again and so he quickly left the police station with Towser at his heels and set out along the waterfront in the hot morning sun. And it was hot, a most unusual state of affairs for the north of Scotland. He pushed his peaked cap back on his fiery-red hair and his hazel eyes saw irritation heading his way in the form of the Currie sisters, Jessie and Nessie.

The eyes of the village spinsters constantly accused him of being a heartless flirt. He touched his cap and said, "Fine morning."

"It is for some. It is for some," said Jessie, who had an irritating habit of repeating things. "Some, on the other hand, are breaking their hearts."

Hamish skirted round them and went on his way. Resentment and self-pity warred in his bosom. He had once helped the Currie sisters out of a dangerous jam and had destroyed evidence to do so. Damn it, he had helped a lot of people in this village. Why should he be made to feel guilty?

His thoughts turned to Angela Brodie, the doctor's wife. Now she had not turned against him. He walked up the short path leading to the doctor's house, went round the back and knocked at the kitchen door. Angela answered it, the dogs yapping at her feet. She pushed her fine wispy hair out of her eyes and said vaguely, "Hamish! How nice. Come in and have coffee."

She cleared a space for him at the kitchen table by lifting piles of books off it and placing them on the floor.

"I don't seem to have had a chat with you in ages," said Angela cheerfully. "Heard from Priscilla?"

Hamish, who had just been lowering his bottom onto a kitchen chair, stood up again. "If you are going to start as well..." he began huffily.

"Sit down," said Angela, startled. "Start what?"

Hamish slowly sat down again. "You haff been the only one who hass not gone on about Priscilla," he said, his Highland accent becoming more sibilant, as it always did when he was angry or upset.

"Oh, I see," said Angela, pouring him a mug of coffee and sliding it across the table towards him. "I only asked about Priscilla because I assumed that you and she were still friends."

"And so we are!" said Hamish. "But ye would-nae think so with this lot in Lochdubh. You would think I wass some sort of Victorian philanderer the way they go on."

"It'll blow over," said Angela comfortably. "These sort of ideas spread through these villages like an infection. Mrs. Wellington started it." Mrs. Wellington was the minister's wife. "She started it by complaining that you were a feckless womanizer and things like that. You know how she goes on. But you brought that on yourself!"

"How?"

"She happened to overhear you doing a very good impression of her to delight the Boy Scouts."

"Ah."

"And so she got a resentment to you and shared it around. Resentment is very infectious. It has always fascinated me the way, for example, one malcontent can bring a whole factory out on strike and keep everyone out on strike until the firm folds and they all lose their jobs. Also, you're going around being so gloomy. That fuels it. You look like a guilty man."

"I'm a bit down," confessed Hamish. "The fact is I've taken a scunner tae Lockdubh and everyone in it."

"Hamish! You love the place!"

"Not at the moment."

"You're due some leave, aren't you? Get right away on holiday. You could get one of those cheap holidays in Spain. Or some of the African package holidays are very cheap."

"I'll think about it," said Hamish moodily. "I might just take a wee holiday somewhere in Scotland, seeing that the weather's fine."

Angela got up and began to rummage through a pile of old magazines on a kitchen chair. She extracted a battered Sunday-paper colour supplement. "What about this place?" she said, flipping open the pages. "Skag. Have you been to Skag?"

"That's over on the Moray Firth. I havenae been there, though I've been into Forres, which is quite close." He looked at the coloured photographs. It looked like a Cornish resort with long white beaches, pretty village and harbour. There was also a page of advertisements for hotels and boarding-houses in Skag. "I'll take this with me, Angela, if you don't mind."

"Keep it," said the doctor's wife. "It's one less piece of junk. I can never bring myself to throw magazines out or even take them along to the waiting-room."

"What's the latest gossip?" asked Hamish.

She sipped her coffee and looked at him in that

vague way she always had. Then she put down her coffee-cup and said, "Well, the biggest piece of gossip apart from yourself is Jessie Currie."

"What about her?"

"Angus Macdonald, the seer, told her she would be married before the year's out."

Hamish's hazel eyes lit up with amusement. "She didnae believe him, did she?"

"She says she didn't, but she's been casting a speculative eye over the men of the village and Nessie is worrying about being left alone."

"And who is this charmer who's going to sweep our Jessie off her feet?"

"Angus will only say it's going to be a divorced fisherman."

"We don't have any divorced fishermen!"

"I pointed that out to Jessie and she said, 'Not yet.'"

"Chance'll be a fine thing," said Hamish. "Dried-up old spinster like her."

"Hamish! That's cruel."

"Aye, well, she should mind her own business instead of ither folks'."

"I really do think you need to get away. Willie Lamont was saying the other day that when you go to the restaurant, you're always complaining about something."

Willie Lamont, Hamish's one-time sidekick, had left the police force to marry a young relative of the owner of the Italian restaurant and worked there much harder than he had ever done when he was a police constable.

"The portions are getting smaller and smaller and the prices higher."

"Still, it's not like you to complain. I'll bet if you had a break from all of us, you'd be very happy to come back and see us again."

Hamish got up. "We'll see. Thanks for the coffee."

He walked along the waterfront and perched on the harbour wall. Towser sighed and lay down. Hamish studied the magazine article. There was an advertisement from a boarding-house called The Friendly House "situated right on the beach with commanding sea views, old-fashioned cooking; special low terms for July, halfboard."

Hamish lowered the magazine and looked over at the village. It was a largely Georgian village, built all in the same year by one of the dukes of Sutherland to enlarge the fishing industry, trim little square whitewashed houses facing the sea loch. He knew everyone in the village, from people who had lived there all their lives like the Currie sisters, to the latest incomers. He felt better now he had talked to Angela, much better. He had been seeing things through a distorting glass, imagining everyone was against him.

So when he saw Mrs. Maclean, Archie, the fisherman's wife, stumping along towards him, carrying a heavy shopping basket, he gave her a cheery smile. "Lazing about as usual?" demanded Mrs. Maclean. She was a ferocious housekeeper, never seen without a pinafore and smelling strongly of soap and disinfectant. Her hair was twisted up in foam rollers and covered with a headscarf.

"I am enjoying the day," said Hamish mildly.

"How ye can enjoy anything wi' that poor lassie down in England eating her heart out is beyond me," said Mrs. Maclean.

Hamish studied her thoughtfully and then a gleam of malice came into his eyes. "Priscilla isn't nursing a broken heart, but some poor fisherman's wife is soon going tae be."

"Whit dae ye mean?"

Hamish slid down from the wall, rolled up the colour supplement and put it in his trousers pocket. "Aye, Angus Macdonald told Jessie Currie she'd be married afore the year was out and tac a fisherman, a divorced fisherman. How's Archie these days?"

"Archie's jist fine," said Mrs. Maclean, her eyes roving this way and that, as if expecting to see her husband. It was well known in the village that Archie, when not fishing, spent most of the day avoiding his wife, in case she scrubbed him to death, as he put it. "Anyway, it's all havers," she said. "Jessie Currie. The very idea."

And then, to Hamish's delight, he saw Archie in the distance. He came abreast of the Curries' cottage and Jessie called something to him over the garden hedge and he stopped to talk to her.

"There's your man ower there," said Hamish happily, "and talking tae Jessie."

Mrs. Maclean stared in the direction he pointed and gave something that sounded like a yelp and set off at speed. But Archie saw her coming and left Jessie and darted up one of the lanes leading up to the back village and was gone from view.

Hamish strolled back to the police station, phoned Strathbane and said he wanted to take three weeks' immediate holiday. Permission was easily granted. The bane of his life, Detective Chief Inspector Blair, was in Glasgow, there had been virtually no crime at all for months, and so it was agreed that Sergeant Macgregor over at Cnothan could take over Hamish's duties as well as his own. He was free to leave at the end of the week. He phoned the boarding-house in Skag and learned to his delight that, thanks to a cancellation, they had one room free for the very time he wanted, and yes, dogs were allowed.

Feeling happier than he had felt for some time, he then set out to arrange for his sheep to be looked after, his hens and ducks as well, and then decided to pay a visit to the seer to find out what had possessed the old sinner to wind Jessie up like that.

Angus Macdonald, the seer, a big, craggy man like one of the minor prophets, peered all around Hamish looking for a present before he let him in. The villagers usually brought him something, a bottle of whisky or a cake.

"No, I didnae bring you anything," said Hamish, following him into his small living-room. "I don't want your services. I simply want to know what you were doing telling Jessie she was going tae marry a divorced fisherman."

"I seed it," said Angus huffily. "I dinnae make things up."

"Come on, man. Jessie!"

"Well, that's whit I seed."

"That sort o' rubbish could start gossip."

"Maybe that's whit you're hoping fur, Hamish."

"How's that?"

"Stop them gossiping about you and your lassie."

"I think you're an old fraud," said Hamish. "I've always thought you were an old faker."

"You're jist bad-tempered because ye think nobody loves ye. Here's Mrs. Wellington coming."

Hamish jumped up in alarm. He scampered off and ran down the hill, seemingly deaf to the booming hail of the minister's wife.

"That man," said the tweedy Mrs. Wellington as she plumped herself down in an armchair. "I'll be glad to see the back of him."

"Is he going somewhere?" asked Angus.

"I met Mrs. Brodie just before I came up here. She said that Hamish was thinking of going over to Skag for a holiday."

"Oh, aye," said Angus. "Now whit can I dae for you, Mrs. Wellington?"

"This business about Jessie Currie. It can't be true." Her eyes sharpened. "Unless you've heard something."

"I see things," said Angus.

"And you hear more gossip than anyone I know," said Mrs. Wellington sharply. "I brought you one of my fruitcakes. It's over on the counter. You see, Mr. Patel at the stores told me that he had seen Archie Maclean talking to Jessie Currie and when he saw his wife at the other end of the waterfront coming towards him, he ran away."

"I'm saying nothing," said Angus mysteriously. "But we'll jist have a wee cup o' tea and try that cake."

* * *

EARLY ON SATURDAY morning, Hamish Macbeth hung a sign on the door of the police station, referring all inquiries to Sergeant Macgregor at Cnothan. He locked the police Land Rover up in the garage, put Towser on the leash, and picked up his suitcase. Then the phone in the police station began to ring. He decided to answer it in the hope that someone in the village might have phoned up to wish him a happy holiday.

The voice of the seer sounded down the line. "I wouldnae go tae Skag if I were you, Hamish."

Hamish felt a superstitious feeling of dread.

"Why not?" he asked.

"I see death. I see death and trouble fur you, Hamish Macbeth."

"I havenae time to listen to your rubbish," said Hamish sharply and put the receiver down.

At the other end of the line, Angus listened to that click and smiled. Called him a fraud, had he? Well, that should give Hamish Macbeth something to think about!

Hamish left the police station and walked along to the end of the harbour to get the bus to Bonar Bridge. From Bonar Bridge he would get another bus to Inverness and then buses from Inverness over to Skag.

The bus was, as usual, late, twenty minutes late, in fact. Hamish was the only passenger. He often thought the driver, Peter Dunwiddy, deliberately started off late so as to have an excuse to break the speed limit, even with a policeman on board. Hamish hung on tightly and Towser flattened himself on the floor of the bus as it hurtled up out of Lochdubh and then began to scream around the hairpin bends on its way to Bonar Bridge. He expected to feel a lightness of heart as Lochdubh and all its residents fell away behind him. But he felt an odd tugging sadness at his heart. To match his mood, the day was grey, all colour bleached out of the landscape, like a Japanese print. He hoped the good weather would return. Perhaps he should not have been so parochial as to holiday in Scotland. When did Scotland ever guarantee sunny weather and water warm enough to go for a swim?

By the time he reached the village of Skag, he felt as tired as if he had walked there. He asked directions to The Friendly House and then set out. It was about two miles outside the village, and not on the beach exactly but behind a row of sand dunes set a quarter of a mile back from the North Sea.

It was an old Victorian villa, vaguely Swiss-chalet design, with fretted-wood balconies and blue shutters. He glanced at his watch. Half past five. Tea was at six.

He entered a dim hallway furnished with a side-table holding an assortment of tourist brochures, a large brass bowl holding dusty pampas-grass, a carved chair, and an assortment of wellington boots. He pressed a bell on the wall and a door at the back of the wall opened and a thick, heavy-set man came towards him. He had blond hair and bright-blue eyes and a skin which had a strange high glaze on it, like china. Hamish thought he was probably in his fifties.

"You must be our Mr. Macbeth," he said breezily. "The name's Rogers, Harry Rogers. You'll find us one happy family here. Come upstairs and I'll show you and the doggie your room."

The room boasted none of the modern luxuries like telephone or television. But the bed looked comfortable, and through the window Hamish could see the grey line of the North Sea. "The bathroom's at the end of the corridor," said Mr. Rogers. "As you see, there's a wash-hand basin in the corner there. Tea's at six. Yes, none of this dinner business. Good old-fashioned high tea."

Hamish thanked him and Mr. Rogers left. Towser, tired after the long walk, crawled onto the bed and closed his eyes. Hamish quickly unpacked, taking out a bowl which he filled with water for the dog, and a can of dog food, a can opener, and another bowl. He filled the second bowl with the dog food and put it on the floor beside the water. Spoilt Towser did not like dog food, but, reflected Hamish, he would just need to put up with it for the duration of the holiday. Of course, maybe he could buy him some cold ham as a treat. Towser was partial to cold ham. He changed into a pair of jeans and a checked shirt, debated whether to wear a tie and decided against it, and then went downstairs and pushed open a door marked "Dining-Room." A small, birdlike woman, who turned out to be Mrs. Rogers, hailed him. "Mr. Macbeth, your table's here...with Miss Gunnery."

Hamish nodded to Miss Gunnery and sat down. All the other diners were already seated. Mr. Rogers appeared and introduced everyone to everyone else. Hamish's quick policeman's mind noted all the names and his sharp eyes took in the appearance of the other guests.

Miss Gunnery on the other side of the table had the sort of appearance which even in these modern days screamed spinster. She had a severe face, gold-rimmed glasses and a mouth like a trap. Her flat-chested figure was dressed despite the humidity of the day in a green tweed suit worn over a white shirt blouse.

At the next table was a man with his wife, a Mr. and Mrs. Harris. Both were middle-aged. She had neatly permed brown hair and neat, closed features, and was dressed in a woollen sweater and cardigan and a black skirt. Her husband was wearing an open-necked shirt and a trendy black leather jacket and jeans, the sort of outfit that tired businessmen in a search for fading youth have taken to wearing, almost like a uniform. He was grey-haired, had large staring eyes and a bulbous nose.

Beyond them were Mr. and Mrs. Brett and their three children, Heather, Callum, and Fiona, aged seven, four, and three, respectively. Mr. Brett was a comfortable, chubby man with glasses and an air of benign stupidity. His wife was an artificial redhead with a petty face and pencilled eyebrows. Either they were plucked, a rare fashion these days, thought Hamish, or they had fallen off, or she had been born that way. She had pencilled in arches of eyebrows, which gave her a look of perpetual surprise.

At the window table were two girls called Tracey Fink and Cheryl Gamble, both from Glasgow. They both had hair sun-streaked by chemicals rather than sunlight and white pinched faces under a load of make-up, and both were wearing identical outfits, striped black-and-white sweaters and black ski pants with straps under the instep and dirty sneakers. And in a far corner was a solitary man who had the honour of having a table to himself. His name was Mr. Andrew Biggar. He had a tanned face and thick brown hair streaked with grey, small clever brown eyes, and a long, humorous mouth.

High tea, that famous Scottish meal now hardly ever served, consists of one main dish, usually cold ham, and salad and chips, washed down with tea. In the middle of each table was a cake stand. On the bottom were thin slices of white bread scraped with butter. On the next layer were scones and teacakes, and on the top, cakes filled with ersatz cream and covered in violently coloured icing.

"Grand day," said Hamish conversationally to Miss Gunnery, for every day in Scotland where it is not exactly freezing cold and pouring wet is designated a "grand day."

Her eyes snapped at him through her glasses. "Is it? I find it damp and overcast."

Hamish relapsed into a crushed silence. He wished he had not come. But Mr. Harris's voice rose above the conversation at the other tables, he of the trendy leather jacket, and caught Hamish's attention.

"Well, this holiday was your idea, Doris," he said.

"I only said the tea was a trifle weak," protested his wife.

"Always finding fault, that's your problem," said Mr. Harris. "If you exercised more and thought less about your stomach, you might be as fit as me."

"I only said—"

"You said. You said," he jeered. He looked around the room. "That's women for you. Always nit-picking."

"Bob, please," whispered his wife.

"Please what?"

"You know." She cast a scared look around the dining-room. "Everyone's listening."

"Let them listen. I'm not bound by your suburban little fears, my dear." His voice rose to a high falsetto. "What will the neighbours think."

And so he went on and on.

The severe Miss Gunnery, who prided herself on "keeping herself to herself," was driven to open her mouth and say to the tall, lanky, red-headed man opposite, "That fellow is a nag."

"Aye, the worst kind," agreed Hamish, and then smiled, and at that smile, Miss Gunnery thawed even more. "Mrs. Harris is right," she said. "The tea is disgustingly weak, the ham is mostly fat, and those cakes look vile. I know this place is cheap..."

"Maybe there's a fish-and-chip shop in the village," said Hamish hopefully. "I might take a walk there later. My dog likes fish and chips."

"Oh, you have a dog? What breed?"

"Towser's a mixture of every kind of breed."

Miss Gunnery looked amused. "Towser! I didn't

think anyone called a dog Towser these days—or Rover, for that matter."

"It started as a wee bit o' a joke, that name," said Hamish, "and then the poor animal got stuck wi' it."

"What do you do for a living, Mr. Macbeth?"

The nag's voice had temporarily ceased. There was silence in the dining-room. "I'm a civil servant," said Hamish. He did not like telling people he was a policeman because they usually shrank away from him. And he had found that when he said he was a civil servant, it sounded so boring that no one ever asked him where he worked or in what branch of the organization.

"I'm a schoolteacher," said Miss Gunnery. "I've never been to Skag before. It seemed a good chance to get a cheap holiday."

"When did you arrive?"

"Today, like the rest. We're all the new intake."

Mr. Rogers and his wife hovered about among the tables, snatching away plates as soon as any diner looked as if he or she was finished. "We have television in the lounge across the hall," announced Mr. Rogers. His wife was carefully packing away uneaten cakes into a large plastic box. Hamish guessed, and as it turned out correctly, that they would make their appearance again during the following days until they had all either been eaten or gone stale.

The company moved through to the lounge. Bob Harris had temporarily given up baiting his wife, but Andrew Biggar made the mistake of asking Doris Harris what she would like to see.

"*Coronation Street* is just about to come on," said Doris shyly. "I would like to see that if no one else minds."

Her husband's voice cut across the murmur of assent. "Trust you to inflict your penchant for soaps on everyone else. How you can watch that pap is beyond me."

Hamish walked over to the television set, found "Coronation Street," and turned up the volume. "I like "Coronation Street,'" he lied to Doris. "Always watch it."

He sat down next to Miss Gunnery. He was aware of the nag's voice all through the programme, sneering and jeering at the characters. He sighed and looked about the room. The chairs were arranged in a half-circle in front of the television set. The fireplace was blocked up and a two-bar electric heater stood in front of it. There was a set of bookshelves containing battered paperbacks, no doubt left behind by previous guests. The Rogerses were probably too mean to buy any. The chairs were upholstered in a scratchy fabric. The carpet was a worn-out green with faded yellow flowers. There were various dim pictures on the walls, Highland cattle in Highland mist, and a grim photograph of a Victorian lady who stared down on all. Probably the original owner, thought Hamish.

At the end of the programme, which he had only stayed to watch for Mrs. Harris's sake, he rose and said to Miss Gunnery, "I'm going to walk my dog along to the village and see if there's a fish-and-chips shop. Want to come?"

"I don't eat fish and chips," she said primly, looking down her nose.

The tetchiness that had been in him for months rose to the surface again. "So you prefer that high-class muck we had for tea?"

There was an edge of contempt to his light Highland voice and Miss Gunnery flushed. "I'm being silly," she said, getting to her feet. "I'd enjoy the walk."

Hamish went up to get Towser, but when he descended to the hall again it was to find not only Miss Gunnery waiting for him but the rest of the party, with the exception of the Harrises.

They did not say anything like "We've decided to come too," but merely fell into line behind the policeman like obedient children being taken for a walk.

Mr. Brett was the first to break the silence. "A

stone's throw from the sea," he exclaimed. "You would need to have a strong arm to throw a stone that distance."

"Are ye sure there's a chip shop, Jimmy?" asked Cheryl. She hailed from Glasgow, where everyone was called Jimmy, or so it seemed, if you listened to the inhabitants.

"I don't know," said Hamish. "May be something in the pub."

"I'm starving," confided Tracey, stooping to pat Towser. "I could eat a horse between two bread vans."

Cheryl slapped her playfully on the back and both girls giggled.

"It's a pity little Mrs. Harris couldn't come as well," said Andrew Biggar. "Don't suppose she gets much fun. Are you in the army, by any chance, Mr. Macbeth?"

"Hamish. I'm called Hamish. No, Andrew. Civil servant. What makes ye say that?"

"When I first saw you, I thought you were probably usually in uniform. Got it wrong. I'm an army man myself. Forcibly retired."

"Oh, those dreadful redundancies," said Miss Gunnery sympathetically. "And us so soon to be at war with Russia again."

"Don't say that," said Mrs. Brett, whose name

turned out to be June, and her husband's, Dermott. "It's been a grim enough start. That man Harris should be shot."

"You can say that again," said Dermott Brett, so June predictably did and the couple roared with laughter at their own killing wit.

"I don't know if I'm going to be able to bear this holiday," murmured Miss Gunnery to Hamish.

"Och," said Hamish, who was beginning to feel better, "I think they're a nice enough bunch of people and there's nothing like a common resentment for banding people together." He winced remembering how common resentment had turned the villagers of Lochdubh against him.

"Harris, you mean," said Miss Gunnery. "But his voice does go on and on and it's not a very big place."

They arrived at the village of Skag. It consisted of rows of stone houses, some of them thatched, built on a point. The river Skag ran on one side of the point and on the other side was the broad expanse of the North Sea. The main street was cobbled but the little side streets were not surfaced and the prevalent white sand blew everywhere, dancing in little eddies on a rising breeze. "Getting fresher," said Hamish. "Look there. A bit of blue sky."

They walked down to the harbour and stood at

the edge. The tide was coming in and the water sucked greedily at the wooden piles underneath them. Great bunches of seaweed rose and fell. Above them, the grey canopy rolled back until bright sunlight blazed down.

Hamish sniffed the air. "I smell fish and chips," he said, "coming from over there."

They set out after him and found a small fish-and-chips shop. Hamish suggested they walk to the beach and eat their fish and chips there.

They made their way with their packets past the other side of the harbour, where yachts were moored in a small basin, the rising wind humming and thrumming in the shrouds. There was a sleazy café overlooking the yacht basin, still open but empty of customers, the lights of a fruit machine winking in the gloom inside.

A path led round the back of the café, past rusting abandoned cars and fridges, old sofas and broken tables, to a rise of shingle and then down to where the shingle ended and the long white beach began.

"You spoil that dog," said Miss Gunnery as Hamish placed a fish supper on its cardboard tray down in front of Towser.

Hamish did not reply. He knew he spoilt Towser but did not like anyone to comment on the fact.

"Why does a woman like Doris marry a pillock like that?" asked Andrew Biggar.

June Brett nudged her chubby husband playfully in the ribs. "They're all saints before you marry them and then the beast comes out."

Dermott Brett snarled at her and his wife shrieked with delight. Faces could be misleading, thought Hamish. June looked rather petty and mean when she was not speaking, but when she did, she became transformed into a good-natured woman. The Brett children were making sandcastles down by the water. They were remarkably well behaved. Heather, the seven-year-old, was looking after her young brother and toddling sister, making sure the little Fiona did not wander into the water. Long ribbons of white sand snaked along the harder damp surface of the sand underneath and then there came a haunting humming sound.

"Whit's that?" cried Cheryl, clutching Tracey.

"Singing sands," said Hamish. "I remember hearing there were singing sands here but I forgot about it."

"It's eerie," said Miss Gunnery. "In fact, the whole place is a bit odd. It never gets dark this time of year, does it, Hamish?"

He shook his head, thinking that the place was indeed eerie. Because of the bank of shingle behind the beach and the flatness of the land behind, there was a feeling of being cut off from the rest of the world. He remembered the seer's prediction with a shudder and then his common sense took over. Angus had heard the gossip about his holiday and had invented death and trouble to pay Hamish back for having called him a fraud.

Miss Gunnery was carefully collecting everyone's fish-and-chip papers when Hamish heard Dermott Brett say, "He's got worse."

"Who?" asked Andrew, lazily scraping in the sand for shells.

"Bob Harris."

"You know him?" asked Hamish.

"Yes, he was here last year."

Miss Gunnery paused in her paper-gathering. "You mean you stayed here and came back!"

"New management," said Dermott Brett. "It was owned by a couple of old biddies. They did a good tea, but their prices were quite high for a boarding-house. We weren't going to come back, because with the three kids it was coming to quite a bit. Then June saw the ad with the new cheap prices, but it said nothing about new management."

"What happened to the old women who owned it?" asked Hamish, ever curious.

"They were the Blane sisters, the Misses Blane.

Rogers said they took a small house for themselves in Skag. Might call on them, if I can find them."

"So Harris is worse now?" pursued Hamish.

"He was bad enough last year, but in fits and starts. Didn't go on like he does now the whole time. Maybe he'll have settled down by tomorrow. Doris Harris wanted to come with us, but he ranted on at her when you were upstairs getting your dog about wasting good money on fish and chips when she had already eaten."

There was a scream of delight from the Brett children. Heather had placed the three-year-old Fiona on Towser's back. Towser was standing patiently, looking puzzled, his eyes rolling in Hamish's direction for help.

"Leave him be," shouted Hamish. Heather obediently lifted Fiona off Towser's back and Towser lolloped up the beach and lay panting at Hamish's feet.

"Time I got those kids in bed," said June. "They've been on the train all day."

"Come far?" asked Hamish.

"From London."

Dermott got to his feet and brushed sand from his trousers. He walked up to the children and swung the toddler onto his shoulders. June joined him, and the family set off together in the direction of the boarding-house.

"That's a nice family," said Miss Gunnery, returning from a rubbish bin on the other side of the shingle, where she had put the papers. "Perhaps we should be getting back as well."

"Whit aboot the night-life o' Skag?" sniggered Cheryl. "Me and Tracey'd like a drink."

"How old are you?" demanded Miss Gunnery severely.

Cheryl tossed her long blonde hair. "Old enough," she said. Her heavily made-up eyes flirted at Hamish. "Aye, old enough fur anything, isn't that right, Tracey?"

"Sure is," said Tracey in a dreadful imitation American accent. "So let's just mosey along to the pub."

"Bound to be bottled beer up here," said Andrew, "but I'm willing to try it. What about you, Hamish?"

"As long as they'll let Towser in."

"He's married tae his dug!" shrieked Cheryl.

Hamish's thin, sensitive face flushed angrily. He was ashamed of his affection for his dog, ashamed sometimes of Towser's yellowish mongrel appearance.

"I think a drink's just what we all need," said Andrew quickly. "Come along, Hamish."

Hamish had a sudden desire to sulk. But Miss Gunnery said, "I saw the pub near the harbour. It looked quite pretty. I think I'll go after all." She linked a bony arm in Hamish's as he stood up and the small party set off.

It was a pretty thatched pub with tubs of flowers at the door, more like an English inn than a Scottish one. But inside it was as plastic and dreary as the worst of Scottish pubs. A juke-box blared in the corner and a spotty moron was operating the fruit machine with monotonous regularity, his mouth hanging open as he fed in the coins. Hamish had noticed a table and chairs outside and suggested they take their drinks there. Cheryl and Tracey had rums and Coke, Miss Gunnery, a gin and tonic, Andrew, a bottle of beer, and Hamish, a whisky and a bag of potato crisps for Towser.

"There's a carnival here tomorrow," said Hamish. "Sideshows and everything. I saw a poster about it on the pub wall."

"I didn't see a fairground," said Andrew.

"It'll be here tomorrow all right," said Hamish, wise in the ways of Highland gypsies. "They come in the night like a medieval army and the next day, there they all are."

They finished their drinks and walked slowly back to the boarding-house. Cheryl and Tracey had decided to compete for the attention of Hamish Macbeth and so they walked arm in arm with him while Miss Gunnery and Andrew followed behind.

When they went into the boarding-house, Hamish collected a couple of paperbacks from the book-shelves in the lounge and went up the stairs to his room.

It was then that he found out that the Harrises had the room next door. Bob Harris's voice rose and fell, going on and on and on, punctuated by an occasional whimper from his wife.

Hamish wondered whether to go next door and tell the man to shut up, but as a policeman he had found out the folly of interfering in marital problems. Doris would probably round on him and tell him to leave her husband alone.

Or rather, that's what the lazy Hamish Macbeth told himself.

VISIT US ONLINE AT

WWW.HACHETTEBOOKGROUP.COM

FEATURES:

OPENBOOK BROWSE AND
SEARCH EXCERPTS
•
AUDIOBOOK EXCERPTS AND PODCASTS
•
AUTHOR ARTICLES AND INTERVIEWS
•
BESTSELLER AND PUBLISHING
GROUP NEWS
•
SIGN UP FOR E-NEWSLETTERS
•
AUTHOR APPEARANCES AND TOUR
INFORMATION
•
SOCIAL MEDIA FEEDS AND WIDGETS
•
DOWNLOAD FREE APPS

BOOKMARK HACHETTE BOOK GROUP
@ WWW.HACHETTEBOOKGROUP.COM